My School Project

FAMILY, FRIENDS AND FURRY Creatures

By Liz Pichon

Scholastic Children's Books
An imprint of Scholastic Ltd
Euston House, 24 Eversholt Street, London, NW1 1DB, UK
Registered office: Westfield Road, Southam, Warwickshire, CV47 0RA
SCHOLASTIC and associated logos are trademarks and/or
registered trademarks of Scholastic Inc.

First published in the UK by Scholastic Ltd, 2017
This paperback edition published 2018

ISBN 978 1407 18679 5

A CIP catalogue record for this book
is available from the British Library.

Printed by CPI Group (UK) Ltd, Croydon, CR0 4YY
Papers used by Scholastic Children's Books are made
from wood grown in sustainable forests.

1 3 5 7 9 10 8 6 4 2

www.scholastic.co.uk

This BOOK is DEDICATED
to my FAMILY

Mark   Zak   Ella   Lily

my FRIENDS

Claudia   Ben

AND

Furry Creatures

SID

When I was at Derek's house, Rooster must have slept on my sweatshirt, because it LOOKS like half his **FUR** coat's on it now!

Normally it wouldn't bother me, but this is an EXTREME **FUR** SITUATION.

Oh...

I know that if Mum and Dad see it they'll start saying things to me like:

"You know Delia's ALLeRGiC to **FUR**, don't you?"

"Why did you let Rooster jump on you?"

"Can't you just stay out of his way?"

(Which is impossible.)

I'd rather stay out of Delia's way, as Rooster's a lot more **FUN** to hang out with.

Woof!

I try and "**SHAKE**" some of the **FUR** off.

But then I remember a TRICK that Mum does using bits of STICKY TAPE wrapped around her hand.

So I get some tape and start patting my sweatshirt up and down like it's a good dog.

I use up HALF a roll of tape trying to get it to work, but most of Rooster's hair is still on the sweatshirt.

So I give up. Sigh.

There are bits of **FURRY** tape EVERYWHERE now. I'm about to get rid of them when another idea **POPS** into my head. ⇒

So I make THESE instead.

My VERY OWN **FURRY**
CREATURES...

(I am a recycling genius.)

Here's a QUIZ.

Is this a **FURRY** CREATURE ...

OR

a **FURRY** FEATURE?

<u>You</u> decide.

(No peeking! Answer on the
next page...) ⟶

FURRY

FEATURE

(HA! HA!)

It's Mr Fullerman with

FURRY NEW HAIR.

Who knew bits of tape and **FUR**
could be **SO** USEFUL?

(I did.)

I have even more **FUN**
sticking some around the house as well ...

... which **M**um isn't too pleased about.

This seems like a good time to do something else that's also VERY important.

Here is a LIST of things I ➡

DON'T want to do:

(In no particular order.)

☹ THINGS I DON'T
WANT TO DO.

Rassspp

1. Wear THESE shoes to school, because they have started to make odd noises when I walk.

2. Be late into class. (See No. 3 for reason WHY.)

3. MISS out on the latest PRIZE for Mr Fullerman's NEW CHART:

NEW chart = NEW PRIZE.
Mr Fullerman told us,

IT'S ⏰ FINE TO BE ON TIME!

Group 1	Group 2	Group 3	Group 4

"'It's Not Great To Be Late' was a BIG success, so I'm offering another PRIZE for the winners of this chart. This will be the LAST ONE we do, though."

I really want to WIN the book tokens and **Whirly BAR** this time. (I bet if Mr Fullerman can think of something else that rhymes with <u>time</u> or <u>late</u> he'll do another CHART.)

(My list continued.)

4. Go anywhere NEAR Amber Tully Jones, who has a stinking cold and keeps *sneezing.*

It's YUCK

5. FORGET to bring in my BABY picture for the NEW school project.

I don't REALLY want to bring ANY of my baby pictures into school ➡ EVER.

But Mr Fullerman said that if we forget them, he'll send a reminder email to our parents, which will be FAR WORSE because Mum checks her emails a LOT and straight AWAY she'll go and find the most embarrassing baby picture she can.

This one's sweet!

Mum:  "LOOK how **CUTE** you are on the potty, Tom."

Me: "Don't SEND that ONE!"

Mum: "TOO LATE."

(I can see it now.)

Writing a list is the EASY bit. Trying to FOLLOW the list is turning out to be a LOT harder than I ever expected.

AGGGHHHH

I tell Mum that I can't wear my shoes any more because they've started to

make embarrassing **NOISES**.

"Every time I take a step a **HORRIBLE** SOUND comes out of my SHOE!"

"Really?" Mum says.

"YES! I thought it was FUNNY at first, but not any more."

"What were you doing?" Mum wants to know.

"JUST WALKING. Look, I'll show you."

I put on the shoes to demonstrate HOW bad the noise really is by stomping up and down the kitchen.

I want Mum to HEAR the FULL RASPING humiliation I had walking home.

"Wait for it..." I warn her.

Mum waits.

"I can't HEAR anything, Tom," she says like I am making a BIG FUSS about nothing.

"HONESTLY, they WERE REALLY NOISY!"

But the only thing we can both hear is me stomping up and down in the kitchen and sighing. I might as well be wearing a pair of fluffy slippers.

JUMPING doesn't help much either.

"They sound fine to me, and I'm not buying you another pair of shoes if that's what you are hoping for."

(It isn't, but it's a good idea.)

"DID you hear that?"

I say to Mum.

"No."

I take my shoes off and start to bend them around to see why they've stopped RASPING.

I should be pleased,

BUT IT'S REALLY ANNOYING.

Mum can see I'm **CROSS**, so she says,

"Take your gym shoes to school, and **IF** the 'NOISE' comes back, you can wear those instead. I'll give you a note."

Which is something, I suppose.

But the way Mum says **IF** makes me think she doesn't really believe me in the first place.

My shoe stomping has taken more time than I expected, so Derek's got fed up of waiting for me outside and knocked on the door.

Stomp Stomp Stomp Stomp
Stomp Stomp Stomp

"HURRY up, Tom! IF we run we might just make it to school on time," he tells me.

Mum puts the note in an envelope and pops it in my bag while I rush around grabbing all my stuff.

Mr Fullerman

Then I sit down and (reluctantly) put my shoes back on.

"Have you got everything?" Mum asks.

"**Y**u**P**, I have EVERYTHING!"

"You haven't forgotten anything important?"

NO!

"Come on, let's GO!"
I say to **D**erek.

We both take a deep breath and start
RUNNING to school.

At first my shoes are OK, but with every STEP the noises get louder.

Huh?

Rrrrrrrraaaaaaassssssppppppppp!

"WHAT is that noise?"

Derek asks me.

"My shoes – just ignore them,"

I tell him.

Which gets harder to do

for both of us.

Rassspppp

Rrrraasssppp

Rrrraasssppp

My shoes make a horrible RASSSSPPPING sound ALL the way to school.

Kids are pointing at me and people are ⊙ ⊙ STARING down at my feet while I pretend that nothing is happening at all.

SHOES!

Check out those shoes.

What's that?

Raassssppp Raasssssppp RaaaSPPP

"They're really noisy, aren't they?"

Derek says, like I didn't know that already.

But then I remember my GYM shoes.

"I FORGOT – I brought spare shoes and a note. I'll put them on right NOW."

I'm SO glad Mum suggested I bring them. ☺

I tip out the **entire** contents of my bag on to the floor. Straight away Derek can tell something is wrong from the l👁👁k on my FACE.

"What have you forgotten?" he asks as I **shake** out my bag some more.

"**EVERYTHING.**"

I've got **NO** gym shoes.

NO note. ➡

NO baby picture.

(So much for trying to STICK to my list.) ☹

"Awwwww... WHY do I **ALWAYS** forget stuff?" I sigh.

Derek tries to be helpful and makes a few suggestions.

"You could try putting your SOCKS over your shoes? That might stop the noise.

Hmmmm

OR why don't you walk in a different way, like on

TIPTOEs?"

Mr Sprocket opens the door and begins

Morning.

RINGING the bell for the start

of the school day.

DING DING

I follow **Derek** inside (on tiptoes) and I'm still

Rrrraasssppping,

just not as loudly as before.

"IT'S working," I whisper. MAYBE nobody will

notice my shoe noises after all. THAT'S what I'm

thinking,  right up until I get to the

corridor...

When everything CHANGES.

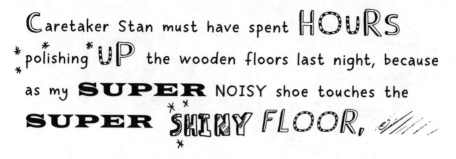

Caretaker Stan must have spent HOURS *polishing *UP the wooden floors last night, because as my **SUPER** NOISY shoe touches the **SUPER** *SHINY* *FLOOR*, I make an even

MORE **SPECTACULAR** SOUND.

(And <u>not</u> in a good way.)

La! La! La! La!

SHINY Floor

Last night in school

RRAASSPPP

EVERYONE looks at ME.

"EWwwwwww."

Was that YOU?

"NO, it's MY SHOES! IT'S MY SHOES!" I say frantically while pointing at them. I make the noise AGAIN to try to PROVE it wasn't ME.

RRRAAASSPPPPP!

The kids all say "TOM!" and lurch away from me.

YUCK

"SHOES! SHOES! SHOES!"

I keep shouting, which doesn't help much.

Brad Galloway thinks it's really funny and makes

things worse by saying, **"GO ON. DO IT**

AGAIN! Make THAT NOISE!"

I can see **M**rs Worthington *LOOMING*

towards me, looking a bit FIERCE.

She's saying, **"WHAT'S GOING ON?**

Who's MAKING ALL THAT NOISE?"**

Before she finds out that it's **ME** I decide to

take OFF my shoes and SOCKS and

make a

RUN for it instead.

Trying not to get my TOES squashed by the oncoming kids isn't easy, but I make it to the classroom in one piece. Now all I have to do is get to my desk without Mr Fullerman SPOTTING my bare FEET.

How hard can it be?

(Very...)

Mr Fullerman sees everything.

I glance down at my toes for a second, just to check they are still there, when Amber Tully Jones walks STRAIGHT into me with her EYES closed ...

ATISHOOOOOO!

... and **sneezes.**

"Thorry, Tom. I didn't thee you.
Mr Fullerman wants us to line
up out-thide."

(At least she has a tissue, which is something.)
She SPLUTTERS past as the rest of
my class begin to file out behind her, forcing me to
protect my FEET even MORE.

Tom!

Norman waves to me and wants to show

off his dance "MOVES" on the

SUPER SHINY FLOOR.

Watch this, he says, and before I can say,

"NO, NORMAN — mind my ..."

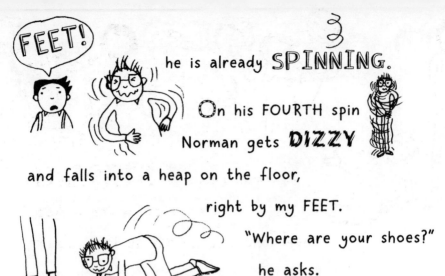

he is already SPINNING.

On his FOURTH spin
Norman gets DIZZY
and falls into a heap on the floor,

right by my FEET.

"Where are your shoes?"
he asks.

Ssshhhhhh! I have shoes, they're just very NOISY. I'll put them back on when I'm in class,

I whisper, trying not to bring attention to my BARE FEET. The MISTAKE I make is WHISPERING, because KIDS pay WAY more attention to what you're saying when you WHISPER.

(That's just a basic school rule.)

TRUE

Norman keeps on STARING at my feet, which makes everyone else LOOK at them too.

"WHY have you got BARE FEET?" Marcus wants to know.

"I have shoes, they're just in my bag," I WHISPER again.

(Another mistake.)

"Aren't your feet cold?" AMY asks me.

"You've got BARE FEET," Solid notices.

Sigh...

Who's got BARE feet?

TOM has.

"Shhhhhhh! Enough about my shoes!"

I try to say as my shoe news

travels all the way up the queue and ...

all the way back down to

Mr Fullerman,

who immediately tells me to put my

shoes back on.

"BUT, SIR, they were making FUNNY NOISES," I try to explain.

"Shoes ON now, Tom," he says, like I have no choice.

(I don't.)

While I'm doing as I'm told,

Mr Fullerman says,

"THANK you, Class 5F. I'm just sorting out a table for your school project. So line up quietly and get your LOVELY baby photos ready because I can't WAIT to see them!"

Mr Fullerman LOOKS at me like he already knows that I've left my picture at home, which makes me feel a bit AWKWARD. I start SHUFFLING my feet from side to side. (Another mistake.) The shoe :RASP: I make is a quiet one (luckily) so Mr Fullerman misses it. Marcus doesn't.

Eeeewwww

"It was my SHOE," I tell him.

I don't want to spend the rest of the DAY every time I MOVE.

RRASSSPING

So I try 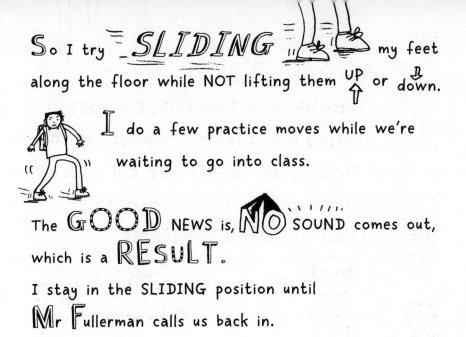 _SLIDING_ my feet
along the floor while NOT lifting them UP ↑ or down. ⬇

I do a few practice moves while we're
waiting to go into class.

The GOOD NEWS is, NO SOUND comes out,
which is a RESuLT.

I stay in the SLIDING position until
Mr Fullerman calls us back in.

You look like a twit.

Thanks!

COME IN, CLASS 5F.

As I'm facing the wrong way, I let the kids go past me.

Marcus wants me to *HURRY UP.*

"Come on, Tom!"

Hurry up!

"After you..." I say as he *SHOVES* past me and RIGHT into Amber Tully-Jones, WHO SNEEZES AGAIN.

MTTISSHOOO

I am nicely protected by Marcus.

Result

I carry on *SLIDING* my feet along the floor one after the other, which still seems to be working.

(No rasping.)

As I *SLIDE* into class, the FIRST thing I SEE is a table full of interesting STUFF.

Mr Fullerman has set out LOTS of CRAFT objects like sticky tape, stars, papers, pencils and glue – all for us to use in our NEW projects. My sliding is useful for taking a GOOD LOOK as I glide past.

I'm not the only one doing it either.

(The LOOKING bit – not the sliding.)

Snot

Slide

Slide

TAPES

I can  HEAR Marcus saying,

THAT ZIGZAG TAPE would be PERFECT for my school project,

which is VERY annoying because I like that TAPE as well.

Along with setting out the craft table,
    Mr Fullerman has also written on the BOARD.

TODAY

we'll be STARTING our NEW
school projects. PLEASE get
out your BABY pictures ready to
put up!

My lack of a baby picture is going to be another problem, I can tell. I'm trying to think of a good excuse...

Photo

Nothing

Photo

... when a BRILLIANT idea leaps into my head. I do a DRAWING of ME as a baby. Then I write underneath,

"REAL photo coming SOON."

This will have to do for now.

Baby Tom

Clever baby

REAL photo coming SOON

"Where's your photo?" Marcus asks me.

"I forgot it, but I'm THINKING this drawing will be OK for now."

"You're THINKING, Tom?"

"Yes, Marcus, I'm thinking.

You should try it sometime."

"Are you thinking right NOW, Tom? Because I can smell BURNING!" Marcus says and sniffs the air.

This is NOT the first time Marcus has done this joke and I ALWAYS pretend not to understand it.

Huh?

"You smell of burning," I say seriously.

"No, not ME - YOU."

"I don't SMELL, so it MUST be YOU..."

NO! NO! NO!

It works every time and drives him CRAZY!

"I can smell burning because your head is WOODEN and you're THINKING - GET IT?"

"NO."

Marcus doesn't give up and KEEPS trying to explain his "joke" to me. (Ha!)

"Can everyone HOLD UP their baby pictures so I can come and collect them?"

(Here goes.)

"SIR! Tom doesn't have a baby photo," Marcus tells Mr Fullerman, helpfully.

"That's TRUE, but I do have this VERY good drawing instead," I explain.
Mr Fullerman tells me he'll send an EMAIL home to make sure I don't forget my photo tomorrow,

WHICH I THINK IS A TERRIBLE IDEA.

NO, sir! I promise I won't forget,

I assure him as I hand over my drawing.

Hopefully I've done enough to persuade
Mr Fullerman NOT to send an email HOME.

(Phew.)

He pins up **ALL** the photos and my drawing.
"Can you tell WHO'S WHO as a baby?" he asks us. Even from a distance I can tell that some kids haven't changed at all.

"**Ha!** That baby picture looks JUST like **Mr Fullerman!**" I say out loud.

"That's because IT **IS HIM,**" **AMY** tells me.

"I knew that..." (I didn't.)

"**W**hich one is **Mr Fullerman?**"

Marcus wants to know.

"Are you serious? Can't you tell?"
AMY says.

(She's got a point.)

aby photos

So far no one has asked WHY I've been *SLIDING* around instead of walking. I've managed to AVOID making any more embarrassing shoe noises, which is a GOOD thing.

Quiet shoes

Avoiding Marcus is almost impossible, especially as I sit next to him.

"What's with the weird *SLIDING* you were doing?"

"It's my shoes. They're making FUNNY noises when I walk. So I'm *sliding*. NO BIG DEAL."

"Is that why you took your shoes off?"

 "YUP." I try to do some more drawing, but Marcus KEEPS talking at me. Sigh...

"**W**hy are your shoes making **WEIRD** noises?"

"I don't know, but that's WHY I'm *SLIDING* everywhere."

"**C**an you show me? **G**o on... Come on, Tom."

"Not now." I ignore Marcus right until he **TREADS ON MY FOOT.**

"**OW!**"

"Sorry. I just want to HEAR your NOISY SHOES!"

"**I**f you stay **OFF** my **FOOT**, I'll try and make the noise - just ONCE - but stop bothering me, OK?"

"**SURE.** Go on, make the noise."

I try to do it softly but nothing happens, so I put my foot DOWN a bit harder.

RRRRAASSSPP.

"Whoaaa..."

Mr Fullerman spins round to see where
the noise is coming from.

I turn and look at Marcus like it's HIS fault.

(Which it kind of IS.)

Marcus, PLEASE don't scrape your chair!

Mr Fullerman says crossly. He HATES the sound of scraping chairs – it's one of the noises that drives him CRAZY. Marcus tries to complain that it wasn't him.

"BUT, SIR!"

Which doesn't work because Mr Fullerman has already moved on and is writing on the board.

"WHAT DID YOU DO THAT FOR?"

Marcus grumbles at me.

"BECAUSE you asked me to!"

He looks so annoyed that I ALMOST feel like making the noise again, just for *FUN*.

I don't, though. (Well, not straight away.)

Uh-oh...

RRRRRAASSSSPPP!

Shoes!

Mr Fullerman comes over to my desk and looks at my shoes.

"Is it YOU making those noises, Tom?"

"Sort of. It's my SHOES. That's why I took them off outside, but you told me to put them back on, so I did, and NOW they won't stop making THAT noise."

I do it again and everyone in the class starts to LAUGH.

RRRRRRRRAASSSSPPP!

"SEE? It wasn't ME making those NOISES!" Marcus says, wanting to get his point over as usual.

"OK, Marcus," Mr Fullerman says, then adds: "Now, as for you, TOM..." Which doesn't sound good AT ALL.

GULP.

But THEN 😊 he sends me down to the school office to see if I can get a pair of gym shoes to wear, just for today.

(They keep sneaky spares so there is no excuse for missing PE.)

No shoes, no PE.

YES you CAN!

Mrs Mumble says, "The ONLY pair I have in your size are **THESE.** ➡️"

She holds up some **VERY BRIGHT WHITE** gym SHOES.

I pretend to be **DAZZLED** by the **LIGHT** of them.

Aghh! I can't SEE! TOO BRIGHT... Can't see!

Which I think is funny.

Mrs Mumble doesn't share my sense of humour. "Just take the shoes, Tom, and HURRY up back to class. Don't forget to bring them back on Monday."

Yes, Mrs Mumble.

I wear my  gym shoes

back to class.

My "I'm **DAZZLED**  by the WHITE SHOES" joke doesn't seem quite so **FUNNY** when Marcus

does it

EVERY TIME HE SEES ME.

Marcus will eventually get bored of being **"DAZZLED"**.

I hope.

My shoe noises have been a bit of a distraction from the NEW school project.

Until **NOW**.

Mr Fullerman hands out a batch of worksheets that are supposed to help us get EVERYTHING finished in time for the school **open day** (which isn't far away). I take a *quick* look to see what I have to do.

Sigh.

The GOOD thing about these worksheets is I can already see there are LOADS of bits I can SKIP over or leave out altogether.

Writing about MY family won't take long - not if I do it like THIS:

Here is my mum ➡️

Here is my dad ➡️

Here is my sister (who's weird) ➡️

See what I mean? EASY! The worksheet does say we should, "INTERVIEW as many of your family or friends as you can."

But that'll take AGES, so I CROSS that out.

~~Interview as many of your family or friends as you can~~

(Sorted.)

As I'm carefully working out what NOT to do for my project, Mr Fullerman CLAPS his hands to get our ATTENTION.

Class 5F – it might SEEM like there's a LOT of worksheets. Some of you might try and skip interviewing your family or friends. PLEASE DON'T as you need to complete ALL the parts of the project. Does anyone have any QUESTIONS?

No skipping work, Tom.

Huh?

Yes, I have one. Are you a MIND READER, Mr Fullerman? I don't say that, but it's what I'm thinking, so he probably knows my question already.

Just in case Mr Fullerman CAN read my mind I decide to at least TRY and PLAN OUT what I'm going to do so I look BUSY. Here are the SIX stages of me carefully working out ...

my SCHOOL PROJECT.

 spots the doodles and stuff I've been crossing out on my worksheets.

"I'm looking forward to this project, aren't you?"

she asks me, which is a SURPRISE.

"YES! Sort of..." I say in a not-very-convincing way. Then I **LEAN** back to relax a bit because I've been working quite HARD already.

"Which EXTRA subject are you going to write about then?"

AMY wants to know.

"WHAT **EXTRA** subject?" I ask.

(I missed that bit.)

"The one Mr Fullerman wants us to choose after we've done the worksheets. You need to pick something you REALLY ENJOY doing, like a hobby. Then write about it for your project," she explains.

"OH, THAT EXTRA subject," I say, pretending I knew all along. (I didn't.)

"I might write about the penguins I've adopted at the zoo," she says.

To: Amy Porter

Which sounds WAY more interesting than anything I can think of.

"Hmmm ... what shall I do?" I wonder.

"There must be something you ENJOY and are interested in," AMY sensibly points out.

There IS, but the only thing that keeps

POPPING into my HEAD IS ...

SNACKS! and eating them...

OH...

OF COURSE! It's one of my favourite HOBBIES. I could write LOADS about that subject. I can SEE it now. Who wouldn't want to read all about the SNACKS I LIKE?

(And some I don't.)

Hoops

Keeps Mum happy

Yeah!

Fee*

Choco Raisins

TOM GATES

GUIDE to

EXCELLENT SNACKS

SNACKS METER

EMERG SNA

WAFER

WAFER

Plain crisp ONLY if nothing else is available.

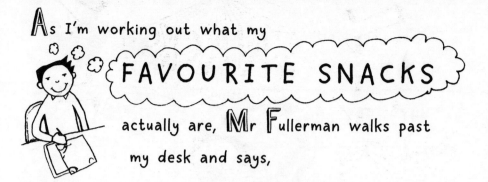

As I'm working out what my

FAVOURITE SNACKS

actually are, Mr Fullerman walks past
my desk and says,

"I'm not sure EATING SNACKS counts
as a hobby, Tom. Is there anything
else you could write about? Have a think."

I say, "YES, sir," but I am a
bit FREAKED OUT because
Mr Fullerman has only gone and done it AGAIN
and READ MY MIND. I nudge AMY and say,
"How does Mr Fullerman ALWAYS seem to know
what I'm THINKING? He's a MIND READER."

"He's not," she tells me.

"He IS," I try to convince her.

"No, he's REALLY NOT..." she says and points out ...

"Oh yeah ... silly me!" I say, trying to cover up how I had no idea I was writing and drawing my thoughts. (It JUST happens.)

"Can you two STOP talking about snacks? It's making me hungry," Marcus grumbles.

"I'm only DRAWING a few snacks, that's all. Here, have a LOOK. Yummy SNACKS mmmmm." I say and WAFT my drawing under his nose.

"NOT LOOKING. Anyway, Mr Fullerman said you need to pick a different subject, REMEMBER?"

I do, and now I'm hungry as well.

I take a quick peek in my bag, hoping to find an emergency TREAT. But the only thing I get is a bit of FURRY TAPE.

"What's THAT? It looks disgusting!" Marcus says. Which gives me another idea...

"This is going to be my EXTRA SUBJECT for my SCHOOL PROJECT,"

I tell Marcus, who doesn't look very impressed at ALL. YUCK.

I've already got a nice collection of these creatures at home, which will be a GREAT START to my work.

If Mr Fullerman asks me WHY I've chosen to write about FURRY CREATURES, I'll say, "Because they are interesting and VERY inspiring, sir." (It's the kind of answer teachers LOVE to hear – especially if you use the word "INSPIRING".)

Very good, Tom.

I like finding out interesting FACTS from the library about all kinds of different creatures as well. It's a good PLAN. WOW!

CREATURES

64

 So I tell Marcus my project's going to be called...

FAMILY,
FRIENDS
AND
FURRY
CREATURES.

 "That bit of tape doesn't look much like a furry creature to me," Marcus says.

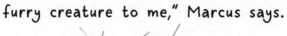

 "Not yet it doesn't..." I agree.

Now it does...

Ha! Ha! Ha! Ha!

(I don't show this to Marcus...)

After not being able to think of anything to do,
I've suddenly got LOADS of ideas. I'm going
to put them ALL in my project for sure.

Especially **THIS ONE**

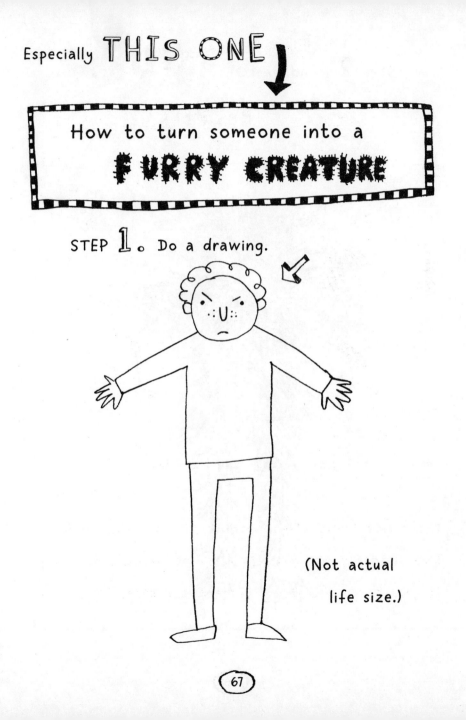

How to turn someone into a

FURRY CREATURE

STEP **1.** Do a drawing.

(Not actual life size.)

Step **2**. Add a LOT of **FUR.**

Result!

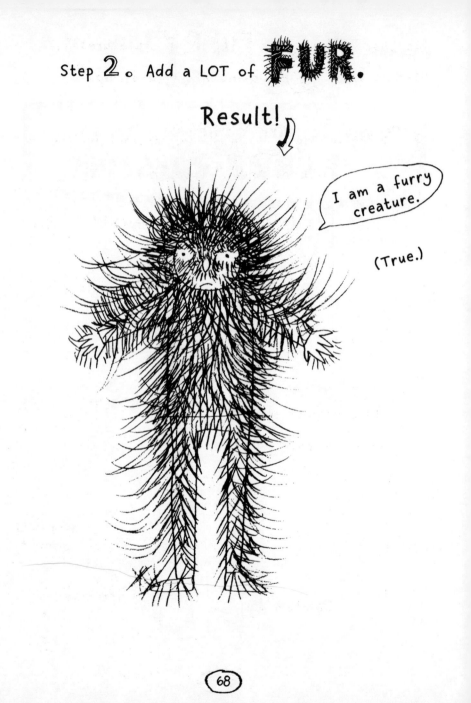

I am a furry creature.

(True.)

"Is that one of your FURRY creatures?" Marcus asks,  looking at my drawing.

 "It is. My WHOLE project will be FULL of them," I tell him.

(He doesn't recognize himself.)

This project is going to be a LOT more FUN than I thought. ☺

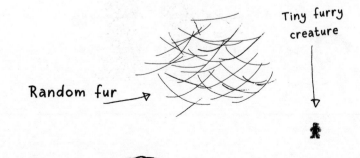

Random fur →

Tiny furry creature
↓

Mr Fullerman CLAPS his hands together again and says he's about to call us up one by one to choose something from the CRAFT TABLE.

"There's PLENTY to go ROUND, so carry on working until you hear your NAME," he adds.

Straight away Marcus says, "I really want that BLUE zigzaggy tape. I hope I get it."

(I hope he doesn't.)

I really want the zigzag tape too.

Then I point out that someone else might get it FIRST. He hadn't thought of THAT. So I make a suggestion.

"If I get called <u>UP</u> before you, I'll take the tape and SHARE it with you. Then you can do the same for me, so we'll BOTH get to have some. That's a good idea, isn't it?"

I don't know WHY I said that because Marcus WON'T agree.

"ARE YOU kidding? No WAY!"

he says. (I knew it.)

Marcus ISN'T great at sharing, and even when he does it's not usually anything NICE.

Mr Fullerman begins to call out names. I am DESPERATE to get chosen, so I put on my "I AM CONCENTRATING and being very GOOD" face and sit up really straight.

Sometimes if I do this FACE at home Mum gets confused and thinks I'm in PAIN. So I try NOT to go too far as everybody wants to get picked FIRST. (Even AMY.)

Pretending to work

Desperate faces

Mr Fullerman begins with...
"UP you go, Trevor." ➡ Yes.

Then Indrani, Yeah!

BRAD, ➡

Solid.

... and it doesn't WORK.

"AMY,

Florence,

then LEROY."

Still desperate →

(There's going to be NOTHING left by the time it's my turn.)

"You're next, Marcus."

NO, NOT MARcus!

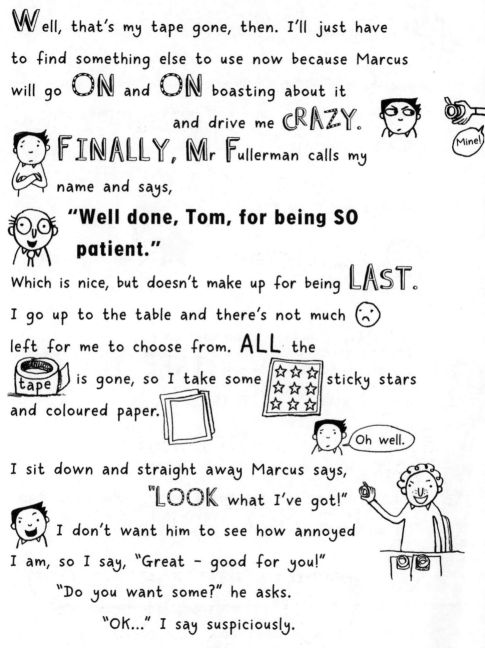

Well, that's my tape gone, then. I'll just have to find something else to use now because Marcus will go ON and ON boasting about it and drive me CRAZY.

Mine!

FINALLY, Mr Fullerman calls my name and says,

"Well done, Tom, for being SO patient."

Which is nice, but doesn't make up for being LAST.

I go up to the table and there's not much left for me to choose from. ALL the tape is gone, so I take some sticky stars and coloured paper.

Oh well.

I sit down and straight away Marcus says, "LOOK what I've got!"

I don't want him to see how annoyed I am, so I say, "Great – good for you!"

"Do you want some?" he asks.

"OK..." I say suspiciously.

I should have known better. Marcus tears off the tiniest bit of tape and gives it to me.
"Don't use it all AT ONCE," he says, LAUGHING.

(Marcus is HILARIOUS...)

"Very funny. I like my STARS, anyway," I tell him.

Then AMY makes a suggestion.
"I'll give you some of my TAPE for some of your STARS," she says, which is very NICE of her. ☺

AMY hands me a pencil with some of her TAPE wrapped around the top and I let her take some stars. It's an excellent SWAP.

"Thanks, this is GREAT!" I say.
(Marcus ignores me.)

He is arranging and ADMIRING all of his TAPES when Mr Fullerman comes over.

"That's rather a LOT of tape you've taken, Marcus." (I agree.)

"Tom doesn't have ANY, so why don't you give him one of yours, PLEASE?"

BUT, SIR! Tom has STARS! ★ ★

"And NOW he has some TAPE." Mr Fullerman just takes one and gives it to ME.

Which makes ME VERY HAPPY! ☺

Unlike Marcus.

Yes!

No!

I will remember the LOOK on Marcus's FACE FOREVER.

My ...
TAPE...

I don't get the zigzag one, but that's fine by me.
To stop Marcus SULKING for the rest of the day,
I give him back the piece of tape he gave me and
a few STARS...

"Don't use the tape all at once!" I add.

Ha! Ha!

HA!

HA! Ha! Ha!

Ha! Ha!

STARTING MY PROJECT

Now I've got my OWN tape - with spots.

(Thanks to Marcus, who still looks a little shocked.)
Mr Fullerman wants us to start planning OUT our projects by writing down some **good** questions to ask our FAMILY and FRIENDS when we do our INTERVIEWS.

Hmmmmmm...

I'm not sure WHAT a **good** question is...

I can think of a few BAD ones, LIKE:

Q: Do you like maths or double maths?

A: NEITHER

But that would make a boring project. Yawn

While I'm working out what to ask I try out my **NEW** tape and ADD a few LINES and STARS, which are very useful for Marcus's SHOCKED look.

TAPE!

My doodling actually helps me to think of a few questions.

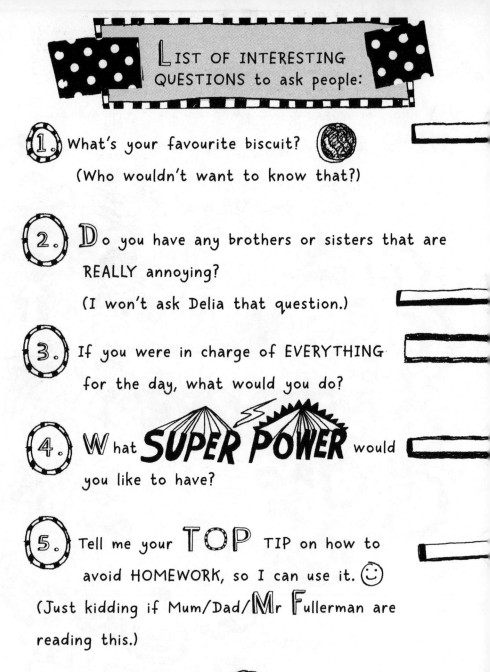

LIST OF INTERESTING QUESTIONS to ask people:

1. What's your favourite biscuit?
   (Who wouldn't want to know that?)

2. Do you have any brothers or sisters that are REALLY annoying?
   (I won't ask Delia that question.)

3. If you were in charge of EVERYTHING for the day, what would you do?

4. What SUPER POWER would you like to have?

5. Tell me your TOP TIP on how to avoid HOMEWORK, so I can use it. :)
   (Just kidding if Mum/Dad/Mr Fullerman are reading this.)

MY ANSWERS would BE:

1. A caramel WAFER followed closely by ANYTHING covered in THICK chocolate or with caramel ANYWHERE.

2. YES I DO! (It's DELIA.)

3. No school (obviously). Everything would be FREE and I could have ANY pet I wanted. My dog!

4. That's EASY – who wouldn't want to FLY?

5. I NEVER avoid homework – I do it all the time. (TRUE.) ☺

Writing down questions and MY answers gets me wondering what other things I could ask...

I can use my school project as an EXCUSE to find out stuff I wouldn't normally get away with from Mum and Dad...

Things like:

You have TWO children — who's your favourite?

I'm not keen on sprouts or cabbage — WHY do you bother giving them to me?

What's your idea of a PERFECT day and would it include visiting Uncle Kevin?

If the answer is YES to the last question, please explain why?

Hmmm...

I've been SO busy writing questions and LISTS that I've missed out on what Mr Fullerman has been showing the rest of the class.

Is everyone clear on HOW to start writing their OWN ...

FAMILY TREE?

(I'm not.)

I've seen a worksheet called "How to START YOUR FAMILY TREE", but it looked very confusing. Everyone else in my class seems to know what to do, so it can't be THAT hard to fill in.

I find my OWN copy and take a look.

I was right...

It IS CONFUSING. 😕 I fill in as much as I can
and then ... I add my OWN extra bits.

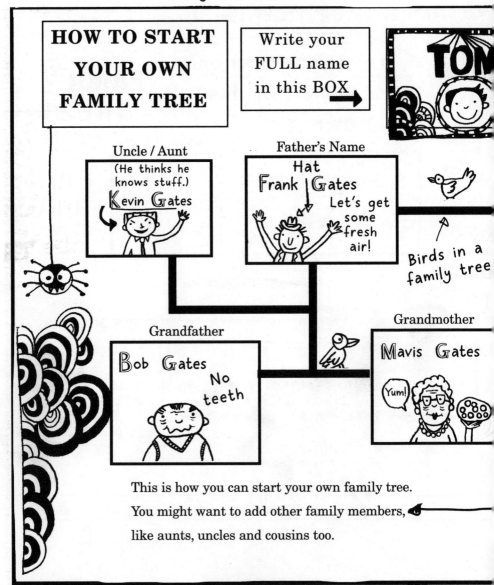

HOW TO START YOUR OWN FAMILY TREE

Write your FULL name in this BOX →

TOM

Uncle / Aunt
(He thinks he knows stuff.)
Kevin Gates

Father's Name
Hat
Frank Gates
Let's get some fresh air!

Birds in a family tree

Grandfather
Bob Gates
No teeth

Grandmother
Mavis Gates
Yum!

This is how you can start your own family tree.
You might want to add other family members,
like aunts, uncles and cousins too.

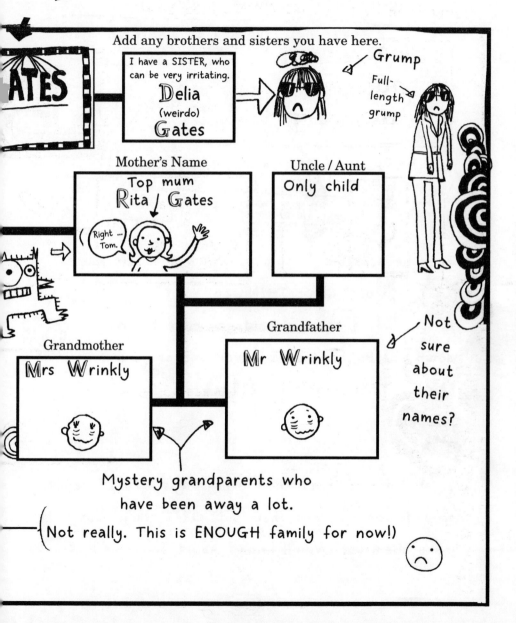

My family Tree is going BRILLIANTLY

when Marcus points at it and says,

You're not supposed to DRAW on that page, Tom.

Oh well...

I've made it more interesting.

Not REALLY.

Then he asks me, "Don't you have a middle name?"

"No, I don't THINK so. WHY?"

"Mr Fullerman said you have to write down the FULL names of everyone on your FAMILY TREE, didn't he, AMY?"

She nods.

"Oh..." I don't know everybody's MIDDLE names, so I decide to leave them out. OR I could just make them up. (Who'll know? Apart from me.)

Mum's parents (my grandparents) are a bit of a mystery. ?

Sometimes I forget I have TWO SETS of grandparents,

THE FOSSILS and the OTHER ones.

I can't remember much about them as they went away when I was little. Dad used to call them The Wrinklies so I've written that down already.

I'm trying to find out if AMY has a MIDDLE name, but I can't quite see. So I ask her and she says...

"I do - it's AMY JAY PORTER.
What's yours?"

"TOM NO NAME GATES," I tell her.

"Of course it is." AMY sighs and rolls her eyes.

Then I notice Marcus has a MIDDLE name as well.

I'm not SURE how to say it, but I give it a go.

 "Orrrrin... Is that your middle name,

Marcus?" I wonder.

"YES - I am an ORIN,"

he tells me proudly, and I start to LAUGH

because it SOUNDS like he just said,

I AM AN ORANGE.

"What's SO funny about that?

I'm NAMED after ORIN Meldrew,

who was a very important person

in my FAMILY a long time ago."

Every time Marcus says ORIN,
it makes me LAUGH - I can't help myself.

Ha! Ha! Ha! Ha! Ha! Ha!

"Sorry, Marcus, it just SOUNDS like you're saying
'I AM an ORANGE'."

"That's not FUNNY," Marcus tells me.

"It's a bit FUNNY," I try and persuade
him, but then Mr Fullerman looks up at
us from his desk.

ENOUGH! is all he has to
say to keep us both quiet.
I'm TRYING really hard to NOT think
about oranges when I notice what
Marcus's WHOLE name spells out, which
sets me off again.
He He HE he he

"Mr Fullerman is looking at us..."

"Did you know that all your names together make you a **MOM?**" I tell him quietly.

Marcus looks at me in a very confused way (which is nothing unusual).

"**W**hat do you mean, 'I'm a **MOM**'?" he repeats.

"**M**arcus **O**rin **M**eldrew. See? You're a **M**.**O**.**M**.," I explain, and then I **LAUGH** because I'm thinking of an orange again.

"Did you just say Marcus is a MOM?" **AMY** asks me.

"That's what his name says. See?"

"Oh yes, so it does."

"I'm not a **MOM**, or an orange, thank you very much," Marcus tells us both. (Even though he is.)

Now it's **AMY**'s turn to look confused.

"I'll explain later," I whisper.

Mr Fullerman stares at me.

"I hope you're discussing your school project. If not,

sssssSHHHHHhhh!"

I go back to my family tree and add a few more doodles around it, which gives me a really good idea for another drawing.

Who wouldn't want to see this?

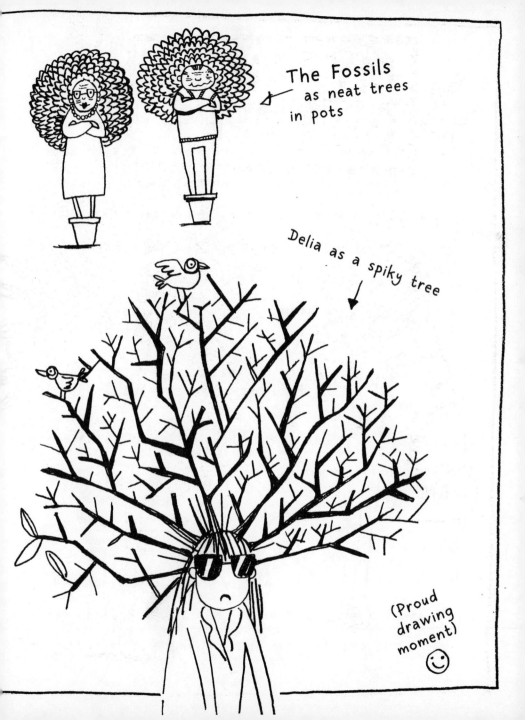

The Fossils as neat trees in pots

Delia as a spiky tree

(Proud drawing moment) ☺

Marcus

AT BREAKTIME,

the first thing I do is go and find Derek to ask
him if he's got a middle name as well.

"I saw you coming from a distance, thanks to
those BRIGHT gym shoes!" he says, which

only encourages Marcus to do his

joke again.

Can't see! The shoes are too bright!

(He'll get bored eventually.)

Then Derek tells me he DOES have a
middle name, which is
NEWS to me.

I don't know WHY, but my parents called me Eric...

"So you're
Derek Eric Fingle?"

"I am. I don't use it much," he says, and I can see
why as it sounds a bit like a poem.

Solid tells us that he's got a middle name too.

I'm Solomon Sam Stewart.

And Norman does as well. (Who knew?)

Mine's Norman Neil Watson.

"Am I the only person who doesn't have a middle name then?" I ask my friends. (They all nod yes.)

"You should just make up your OWN name!" Norman suggests.

Hmmmmm

We spend the rest of breaktime thinking of middle names for everyone, even if they've got one already. Just for ☆FUN.☆

Names   Names   Names   Names

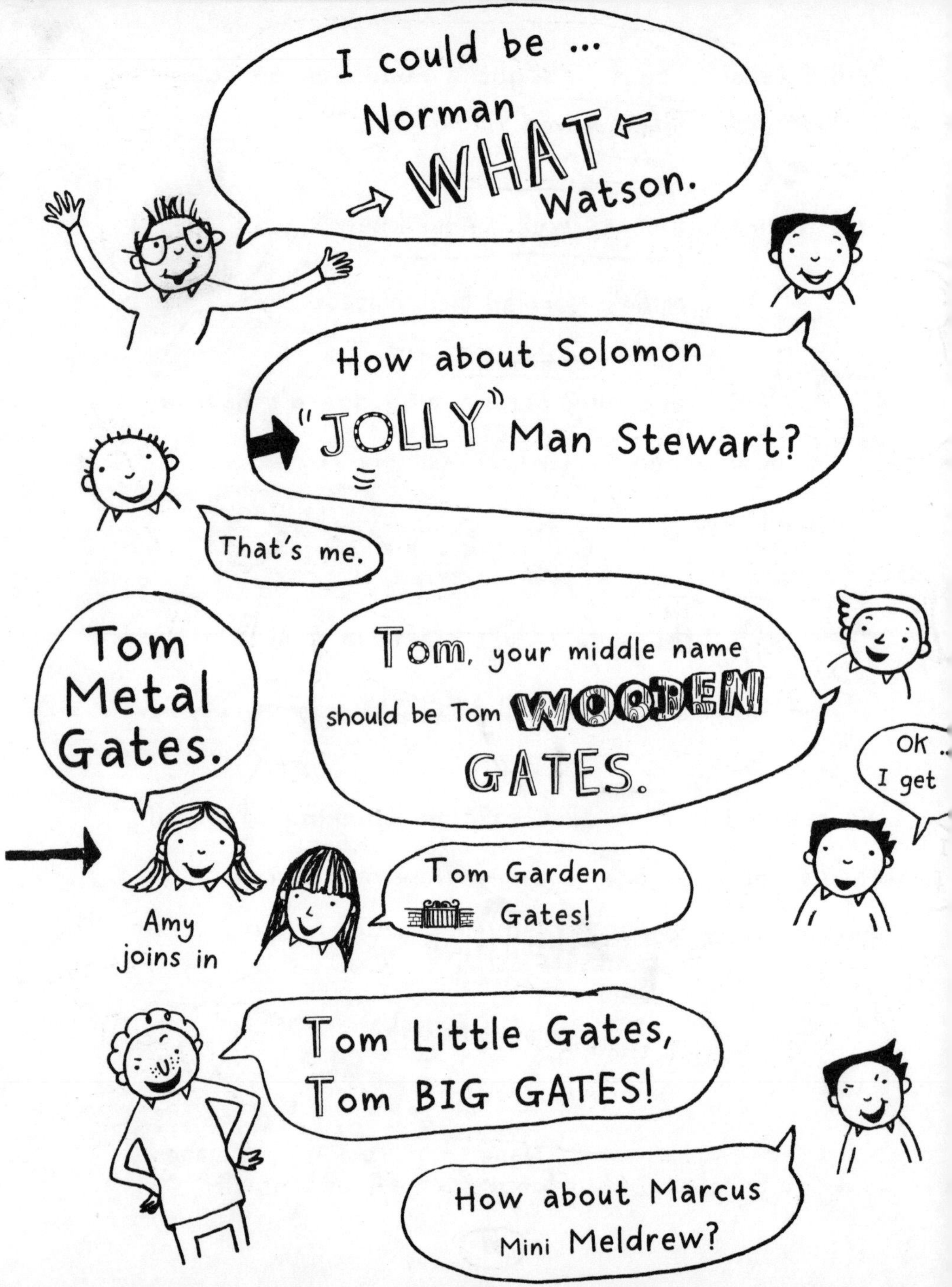
I could be ... Norman WHAT Watson.
How about Solomon "JOLLY" Man Stewart?
That's me.
Tom Metal Gates.
Tom, your middle name should be Tom WOODEN GATES.
OK .. I get
Amy joins in
Tom Garden Gates!
Tom Little Gates, Tom BIG GATES!
How about Marcus Mini Meldrew?

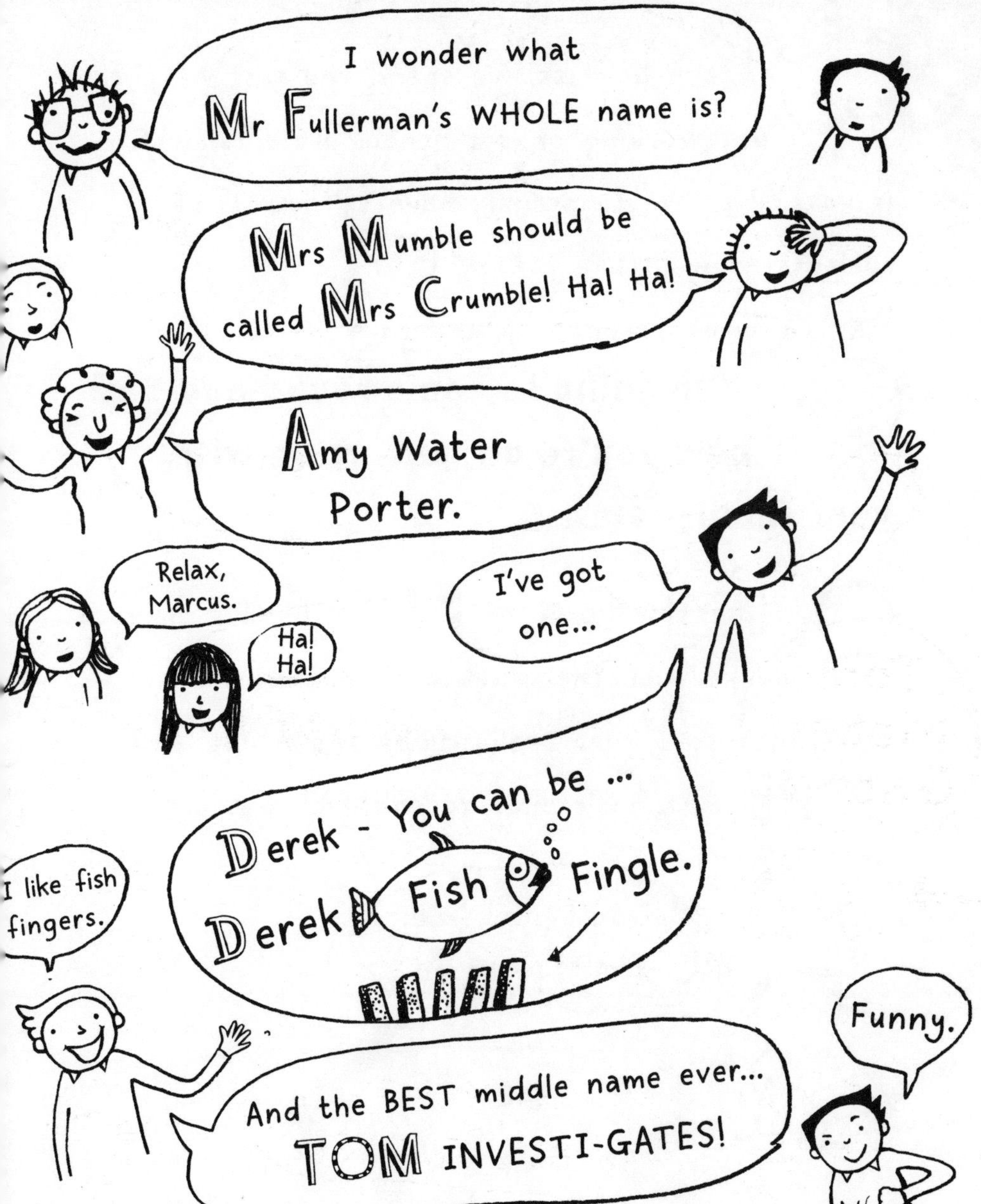

(I'm quite glad I don't have a real one now!)

Back in class, we spend the rest of the day working on our school projects, which is unusual as we'd normally have to do OTHER subjects as well (like MATHS 😖).

Mr Fullerman stands up and says,

"I'm going to come round and SEE how you're all getting on with your family Trees."

I don't want to be FIRST this time (unlike with the craft table – that was different), so I keep really quiet and STILL and HOPE Mr Fullerman doesn't pick me.

Don't pick me, don't pick me...

(Which doesn't work.)

"How's your family Tree going,

Tom?" he asks. I show him the REAL one

(not the picture of my family @S trees).

"This is a GOOD START, though I'm
not sure your grandparents are called
the Wrinklies, are they?"

"I don't know their real names,"

I explain. "My dad calls them that."

"Well, I'm sure your parents could
help you fill in the names. I can add
that to the EMAIL I'm sending them."

(NOT THE EMAIL HOME AGAIN!)

I thought I'd stopped this happening already.

This time I try saying how busy my parents always are.

"They don't have <u>any</u> time to read emails, sir.

And it's mostly my sister's fault."

"Your sister?"

"Yes, she's VERY difficult and takes

up a lot of their time."

(I haven't really thought this excuse through, but it seems to be working, so I keep going.)

"If my mum and dad aren't all STRESSY about Delia, I'll ask them to help me," I tell Mr Fullerman, and he looks convinced.

"OK, Tom, that's fine," he says and moves on to looking at **AMY's** and Marcus's projects.

PHEW!

I think that worked.

I'm going to use Delia as an excuse again, that's for sure.

"Delia ATE my homework."

"Sorry I'm late, sir - it was Delia's fault."

"OK, Tom, I understand."

The **LESS** Mum and Dad know about my project, the better.

Otherwise I won't get to have my *relaxing* weekend, and I'm really looking forward to THAT.

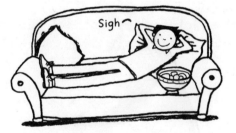

After what feels like a VERY long day at school I get home to find Mum's left a note on the table (along with a few other things, too).

I'm guessing Mr Fullerman sent that email after all.

(I'm still not bringing any of these baby pictures into school though.)

The Weekend

When I wake up 👀 my **plan** is to spend as much time as possible doing these things:

1. *Relaxing.* ☺

2. Hanging out with **D**erek.

3. **E**ating the [last] crumpets* I've hidden so Delia can't pinch them.

Delia

(This <u>won't</u> happen)

Hidden crumpets

The CRUMPET part of my plan works out OK (the rest of it, not so well).

*Crumpets are delicious bread-like things that you TOAST and eat warm with butter. Yum yum.

"Did you just eat the LAST crumpet, Tom?"

Delia asks me crossly.

"If you SNOOZE

YOU LOSE,"

I tell her in case she needs reminding how delicious

crumpets are. "Yum yum."

"YOU are an idiot," she tells me, which

is clearly NOT true.

"I think you'll find I'm ACTUALLY very smart,"

I say in between mouthfuls of crumpet.

(I can't wait to tell Derek how cross Delia is at

missing out on the crumpets!)

Then Mum and Dad walk in and the first

thing Mum says is,

RIGHT...

(Which is never a good sign.)

She NEVER follows it up with something NICE like...

Right ... let's go and get *ice cream.*

OR...

Right ... you can watch TV for as long as you want.

It's ALWAYS...

Right ... time for BED, Tom.

Right ... let's cut your toenails.

This time she says,

"RIGHT ... I've had an email about your school project and your shoes too."

Mum holds up a piece of paper that's been printed off the computer.

Subject: Tom's homework (and shoes)
From: Fullerman, Mr
To: Gates, Rita; Gates, Frank
Sent: Friday, 7:21 p.m.

Dear Mr and Mrs Gates,
Tom's shoes were making unusually loud noises, so he's been lent a much quieter pair of gym shoes to wear. On Monday, he'll need to bring:

- The gym shoes back
- A NON-noisy pair to wear
- A lovely baby picture for his school project

Tom's made an excellent start to his family tree, but needs a little help filling in some parts of it. Attached is a list of all the work we'll be doing (in case it gets lost!). Tom seemed to think you would be FAR too busy to help him! I'm sure that's not the case.
Thank you for your support.

Kind regards,

Mr Fullerman

"Mr Fullerman mentioned your noisy shoes, so we'd better find you a different pair this weekend."

"OK..." I say.

"And I've got a list of everything you'll need to do for your school project, so you won't forget anything."

HA!

"Great," I sigh. Delia starts LAUGHING because she can tell I'm not happy.

"I don't know WHY Mr Fullerman thought we wouldn't have time to help you," Mum says.

(I keep quiet.)

Getting EMAILS from school is making it a lot harder to avoid homework.

"**H**e also wants us to help you finish off your **FAMILY TREE**," says Mum.

"**W**e never had projects like this when I was at school," Dad adds.

"Lucky you..." I mutter.

I have no idea WHY Mum and Dad are taking **SO** much interest in MY school project. They don't normally - not like this anyway.

We're keen!

"You can do my project for me if you want," I tell them hopefully.

Nice try, Tom...

"It'll be good to get it done NOW, just in case," Dad says cheerily.

"In case of WHAT? It's the weekend. Are we doing something SPECIAL?" I ask, as I can feel my *relaxing*  weekend disappearing.

Mum doesn't take any notice of me and says, "Let's see what you've done so far."

I have to go and get my project or they won't let me go to Derek's. I'm sure about that.

For some reason, Delia is still hovering in the kitchen like a **DARK** cloud. You'd think she'd have something better to do. Given half the chance, I wouldn't be here – I'd be with Derek.

"This school project doesn't HAVE to be finished for a VERY long time," I tell Mum and Dad so they KNOW I don't have to do it TODAY.

So much time!

They ignore me and start looking at my school project (so far). Especially my FAMILY TREE.

"Interesting names, Tom," Dad tells me.

"Don't you know what your grandparents' REAL names are?" Mum wants to know.

I thought I did.
Dad calls them
The Wrinklies.

"HA! The Wrinklies! I haven't heard that for a while!" Dad LAUGHS.

Then Delia BUTTS in because she's STILL HERE.
"He was only small and annoying when they left, so why would he remember anything?"

"I thought he'd remember their names," Mum says.

"Errr ... HELLO? I am HERE, you know! And I do remember some things about them. Just not EVERYTHING," I say, because some memories are coming back to me.
(One in particular springs to mind.)

114

"I can remember a VERY small dog they had. I always wanted to stroke it, but for some reason I wasn't allowed."

"I'll tell you WHY! That dog BIT me once, and it used to BARK all the time!"

Yap Yap
Grrrr
Yap

Oh, yes... So it did. That's why we wouldn't let you stroke it, Tom.

"You let me, though,"

Delia tells Mum (proving to me that I am the FAVOURITE CHILD, although I don't SAY it out loud).

Then Dad says, "See, Rita – they DO remember some things about your parents!"

I'm about to ask another question when Mum interrupts me.

"Do you know WHERE ..."

"... Your grandparents are?"

 "No. Where the DOG is NOW?"

(It's not the question Mum's expecting.)

 "Oh... They couldn't take the dog travelling with them, so I'm sure they found it a lovely new owner and home."

Which is a shame because we could have looked after it.

 Did you bite Delia, then...?

"Your grandparents still send letters and postcards and keep in touch whenever they can."

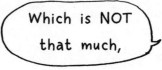 Which is NOT that much,

Delia chips in.

 "They don't really do modern technology," Mum tries to explain.

"Do you mean 'MODERN TECHNOLOGY' like a phone?" Dad mutters quietly.

"You KNOW what I mean. They don't have mobiles and they can NEVER remember people's numbers, so it's just easier to write."

"When was the last time they sent a postcard?" Dad asks.

"LAST week, actually. AND they sent a photo too."

"Of a DOG?"

I ask, as they seem to like dogs.

Cheese!

"No, not a dog, but they have seen some VERY interesting animals on their travels," Mum tells me.

Hi.

"So will they EVER come back?" I wonder.

"They didn't EXACTLY say, but they might visit quite soon. They're missing home and all of US a lot," Mum says.

"REALLY?" Dad LAUGHS like he doesn't quite believe it.

"YES, Frank, that's what they said." Mum sounds like she's getting a bit annoyed. So before she gets TOO cross, I throw in what I think is another IMPORTANT question.

"IF they come back, does that mean I'll start to ..."

 " ... get to know them MORE? I hope so," Mum interrupts me again.

" ... get **MORE** birthday presents, with double grandparents and everything?"

"Typical Tom,"
Delia says in the background.

"I'm just ASKING, that's all," I add.

If they **DO** come home, this could be a **BIG ↕ BONUS** for me.

They might even get another dog, which would be ALMOST like having my <u>own</u> pet. I'd be able to take it for walks too.

While I'm imagining a dog,
Mum goes back to my school project.

"Let's get some work done, shall we?
Who wants to see a PICTURE
of my parents?"

We all do.

"Come on, Frank, you can help me find the picture."

"Can I?"

"Take the hint, Dad. Mum wants to talk to you," Delia tells him.

"We won't be long," Mum says as they leave.

"Mum's got something to say about her parents that she doesn't want us to hear," Delia says.

She seems very sure about that.

While they're gone I ask her more about the dog.

When you got bitten by their dog, did it hurt?

"OF COURSE it HURT!
What kind of question is THAT?"

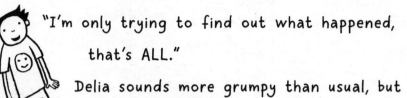

"I'm only trying to find out what happened,
that's ALL."
Delia sounds more grumpy than usual, but
I keep going and ask her something ELSE.

"Why did our grandparents go away in the
first place?"

"If I tell you, don't go BLABBING to
Mum and Dad about it, OK?"

"OK." I have to agree or she won't tell me
ANYTHING.

"When you were a baby, and only slightly
less annoying than you are now," Delia starts
to tell me.

"You're annoying as WELL," I remind her.

Do you want me to carry on or NOT?

"Yes - go on, then..."

They retired from teaching and sold up everything to go travelling - including their house, which Mum only found out about once they'd left. She thought they'd be gone for a few months. SEVEN years later, they're still away, having **ADVENTURES** all over the world, like swimming with sharks.

"We should go on **ADVENTURE** holidays. I'd LOVE that," I say enthusiastically.

"I wouldn't - remember when we stayed in the WRONG mobile home for a week? That was BAD enough," Delia reminds me.

(This is the longest Delia has EVER spoken to me for.)

122

I know a bit MORE about my grandparents now...
Unless Delia's just making things up.
She's done THAT before.

Now Delia starts being NOSY about my project.

"Am I in your project then, Tom?"

"Not much. I want good marks for it."

"VERY funny," Delia says.

Pleased face "I'm not interviewing Uncle

Kevin and Aunty Alice, and I'm leaving

out the cousins completely, so you should be pleased

you're in it at all. I don't want to make TOO much

extra work for myself," I explain.

I look at my FAMILY TREE again (both versions) as Mum and Dad come back from their "chat". Mum hands me a photo. "This is an old picture of your grandparents," she tells me.

They don't look how I expected at all, especially after what Delia told me.

WOOF WOOF
WOOF WOOF

I can't imagine them swimming with sharks.

"Is that the DOG that bit Delia?" I ask.

"It might be..."

"This was taken BEFORE they both retired as teachers and SET OFF around the world," Mum explains.

"I KNOW! Delia said they sold their house and went off to have LOADS of ADVENTURES, which sounds AMAZING!"

"Did you SAY that, Delia?" Mum looks around but Delia's already LEFT.

I forgot she didn't want me blabbing about it.

Oh well.

Then Dad joins in with the conversation.

"It's TRUE, they did swim with sharks, but the sharks were more SCARED of them!"

He LAUGHS while Mum gives

him a LOOK.

AGGH!

Hi!

"Your dad's just being SILLY."

Just in case, I'm going to leave some SPARE PAGES in my project to ADD any other interesting stories I might find out about them (even if it is more work).

"So WILL they EVER come home?"

I ask Mum and Dad.

"EEErrrr... They might.
You never know, it could be
sooner than you expect," Mum
tells me. "In the meantime WE can
help you with your project, and I'll tell you some
other good STORIES – LIKE how your mum and I
MET!"

 (I groan...)
Then Mum says that word.

RIGHT...

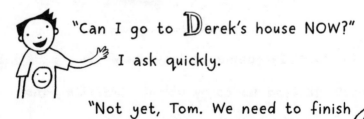 "Can I go to Derek's house NOW?"
I ask quickly.

"Not yet, Tom. We need to finish
off your family tree, THEN go OUT to get
some NON-noisy shoes!" Sigh.

Mum starts READING my work and gets to the
few lines I wrote about Delia.

 "You might want to say something nicer about
your sister here..."

"Hmmmm, not really. It's all TRUE."

Then she writes down a LIST of names.

 "Here's your grandparents' **FULL** names
and you can keep this photo too."

Petula Rita
BARK

Tony
John
BARK

"BARK? Is that their surname?"

"It used to be mine too. I didn't mind
changing it!" Mum tells me.

"There's ONE other missing name that I really
want to know," I say.

"What's that?"

"**W**hat <u>WAS</u> their **DOG** called?"

(It's an important question, I think. But no one
can remember.)

Nipper? ——→   Grrrr   Fang? ←

They carry on discussing <u>MY</u> school project until
Mum notices the time. She wants us to go out and
get my non-noisy shoes.

What's Uncle
Kevin's middle
name?

Sigh.

These family
interviews look
interesting!

I do a GOOD job of persuading Mum to let Derek come with us.

Pleeeease ...
I can go and see him now.

I'm sure Derek won't mind coming shoe shopping and helping me out.

After all he is my

BEST FRIEND.

SHOE SHOPPING, are you **KIDDING?** I HATE shoe SHOPPING. Do I have to come with you, Tom? 😣

"No one likes SHOE SHOPPING. But I have an excellent **PLAN** that's going to take us right ⟹ *PAST* the NEW

ice-cream parlour.

If you're with me, Mum won't mind letting us try it out."

YES!

Derek likes my plan, but he likes *ice creams* more.

(We both do.)

We have half an hour before Mum wants to leave, so playing with Rooster seems like a VERY good use of time.

While we're throwing a ball, I tell Derek all about my OTHER grandparents, and he thinks they sound interesting as well.

"They were teachers and NOW they leap out of planes, swim with sharks and have ADVENTURES."

"They don't look like they'd have **ADVENTURES**."

They look like they'd have early nights and drink tea," I tell Derek.

"That's INTERESTING..." he says.

"Is it?"

"Yes! Are they quite secretive as well?"

"I don't know much about them, if that's what you mean," I explain.

"Even MORE interesting. I think your grandparents COULD be SPIES."

"Really - how come?"

"Because I'm reading a really good book with SPIES in it, and THEY swim with sharks and jump out of planes as well."

"**W**hat do SPIES look like, then?"

"Like ordinary people who don't want to

STAND OUT."

Which makes sense.

"Maybe your mum and dad don't even know they're SPIES. They could be on a SECRET mission," **D**erek suggests.

I hadn't thought about that at all. **D**erek's got me thinking.

"You'd get good marks for your school project if you had REAL SPIES in it!" he adds.

While we've been talking, Rooster's found a pile of grass cuttings to *ROLL* in (which he does ... A LOT).

Rooster looks even more **FURRY** now.

I ask Derek if he can take a photo so I can put it in my school project, which confuses him. "How does Rooster fit in with SPIES?"

"My project's on FAMILY, FRIENDS - that's you by the way - AND all kinds of **FURRY** creatures. I'll show you." I pick up some bits of grass and demonstrate what I mean.

"Look, I'm a **FURRY** creature ... or Mrs Worthington!"

Derek LAUGHS and takes a photo of me as well.

W hich gives me another idea... I collect up MORE grass cuttings and save them in an empty crisp packet for later. I can hear Mum calling us from the garden as she's ready to go shopping.

> T OM! Time to come home now. I'm ready to go.

D erek looks as KEEN as I am to buy shoes.

"Think of the *ice cream*," I remind him, which keeps us going.

(The photo of Rooster cheers us up.)

SURPRISINGLY we find the right (non-rassssssping) shoes in **NO** time at all, which is a **HUGE RELIEF,**

That was quick!

Yes.

THESE!

AND they even fit me as well.

SALE

Mum is very pleased I've found a pair in the **SALE.** "I love a bargain." She smiles. All I have to do **NOW** is persuade her that a trip to the *ice-cream* parlour is also an excellent idea.

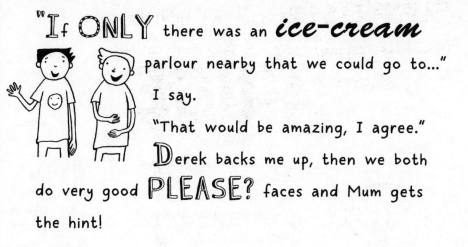

"If **ONLY** there was an *ice-cream* parlour nearby that we could go to..." I say.

"That would be amazing, I agree." **D**erek backs me up, then we both do very good **PLEASE?** faces and Mum gets the hint!

"OK, you two, let's go." Which is another **BIG** result!

HIGH FIVE!

But all my speedy decision-making instantly disappears when it comes to *ice cream.*

Hmmm...

Choosing what flavour to have is HARDER than anything else we've done so far.

It takes a while, but I go for vanilla with caramel *swirls.* Derek picks chocolate. Mum always has the same flavour - PEPPERMINT -  which shouldn't really be an *ice cream,* if you ask me. (It's the only flavour I don't like ... SO FAR.)

"It's delicious," Mum tells us.

"It's not..." I whisper.

As we're walking out of the shopping centre, Derek and I both spot a

photo booth.

I know we've already had *ice cream,* but I'm going to ask anyway. Or, in this case, do LOUD HINTING.

Do you know WHAT WOULD HELP ME WITH MY PROJECT?

No, Tom, what?

IF I HAD A **photo booth** PICTURE WITH YOU - MY BEST FRIEND - TO PUT IN MY SCHOOL PROJECT. HOW GOOD WOULD THAT BE?

LOOK OVER THERE... A **photo booth!**

(So there is...)

"You two! I get the message. We can do some photos, but only because the shoes were on sale."

Derek and I do an *ice-cream* high five.

Yes!

Derek says he's glad he came with me now.

I've done this type of photo before, but only for OFFICIAL things like my PASSPORT. You're not allowed to smile or eat *ice cream* in those pictures. Delia had to take off her sunglasses for hers and wasn't happy at all, which is NORMAL for her.

My
passport
← photo

Extra-
cross ⟹
Delia

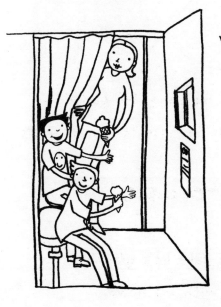

"Don't put the money in until your stool is at the RIGHT HEIGHT. Can you see yourselves, boys?" Mum asks before she pulls the curtain.

"Yes!" I say...

But the FLASH goes off too *fast*.

Mum says we can do some more and she'll help us this time...

Only she doesn't.

"This is the LAST set – I'll stay out this time,"
Mum says, wiping *ice cream* off her face.

These pictures are even better than the last ones.

We head back home after a successful shopping trip (which is unusual). Derek goes back to his house and I FINALLY get to *relax*, which I do while wearing my brand-NEW (non-rasssping) shoes, on my nice, comfy bed.

I'm eating a chew bar I SAVED, while l👀king at the ceiling and wondering if I'll EVER be allowed to DRAW on it? It would look really good if I could, though it might be tricky to do.

Then Mum opens the door ...

JUMP!

... and makes me

I try to hide my chew bar.

"TOM!

Your Uncle Kevin's here.

Can you come down and say HELLO?"

"Do I **waft** to?" (It's hard to talk

with a mouth full of chew.)

"Yes. And please don't take **AGES** either."

"Awwwwww....."

When Uncle Kevin comes round unexpectedly,
Mum and Dad say things like,

What a NICE surprise!

But I'm not entirely sure they mean it. I go
downstairs (after finishing the chew bar) and I can
hear them chatting.

Dad's saying,

We weren't expecting to see you
today, Kevin!

"I sent you a message earlier –
didn't you see it?" Uncle Kevin asks him.

"Sorry, I must have missed it. I've been
VERY busy," Dad says, looking at his
phone. (Sometimes Dad ignores messages
depending on who
they're from.)

Your phone's got a message, Dad...

Nothing important.

"Hi, Uncle Kevin,"
I say in a cheery way, even
though my *relaxation* has been disturbed.

"Hi, Tom! What have you been up to
then?" Uncle Kevin wants to know.

Before I can say, "I was trying to
relax,"

Mum answers for me.

"Tom's been working very hard on his school
project of a FAMILY TREE..."

"That's a thought, Tom – **WHY** don't you go and bring your project down so Uncle Kevin can help with the names you weren't sure about?"

"You didn't know them either!" I point out. "Uncle Kevin doesn't want to see my schoolwork, Mum..."

"I would LOVE to!"
(Groan.)

"OFF you go. CHOP! CHOP!" Mum says, trying to be encouraging (which makes me want to walk even slower).

I go BACK upstairs and bring my project down. Uncle Kevin explains why he came over.

"I REALLY need my POWER DRILL back to put up some pictures. The one I lent you a while ago."

Dad looks puzzled.

"Are you SURE it's YOUR power drill? I thought it was mine. Didn't I lend it to YOU?"

"It's a top-of-the-range EXPENSIVE power drill. It's DEFINITELY mine."

(This could take a while, so I try and sneak out, which doesn't work.)

"TOM, stay here, this won't take long." Mum puts her hand on my shoulder.

(Uncle Kevin and Dad often disagree about stuff – it happens a LOT.)

I know it's mine, Frank.

I'm not so sure ... but I'll go and find it...

Dad goes off to look for what he's SURE is HIS power drill while Uncle Kevin talks to Mum. "It's definitely mine, Rita."

 "If you want to help Tom with his FAMILY TREE I'll go and help Frank find 'THE' power drill," Mum says, and OFF she goes.

"Right, Tom, let's have a look." Uncle Kevin starts making "Hmmmmm" noises and crossing things out, which doesn't sound good.

Another noise that I don't want to hear is Delia coming back, but she walks in at EXACTLY the wrong moment.

"Hello, Uncle Kevin – what are YOU doing HERE?" she asks, slightly surprised.

"I'm picking up **MY** power drill and HELPING Tom with his FAMILY TREE," Uncle Kevin tells her. "IF Frank hasn't LOST it – he's been gone for a while!"

"OH, the FAMILY TREE! How's it going, Tom?" Delia wants to know, which makes me SUSPICIOUS.

"Fine – why?" I ask.

"So, Uncle Kevin, has Tom asked you to be part of his project yet? Because he told **ME** he really wanted to interview YOU and Aunty Alice as well. Didn't you, Tom?" 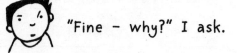 Huh?

(Delia is ONE sneaky sister. She **KNOWS** I didn't want to do LOADS of EXTRA work!)

"It's FINE, Uncle Kevin. I don't need to interview everyone," I point out quickly.

"I'd LOVE to be part of your project, Tom. I have LOTS of good stories to TELL!"

(Whhhaaaaatttt?)

"LOOK at Tom's HAPPY little face! Told you Uncle Kevin wouldn't mind!"
Delia knows this is driving me CRAZY. My sister is so ANNOYING. If there was a chart of annoying people, she'd be right at the top.

Hello, I'm Delia and I'm annoying.

SO annoying

Mostly annoying

Can be annoying

Most annoying person ever

Regularly annoying

Tom!

Yowl Yowl

Ha! Ha!

Then Uncle Kevin looks at his watch and says, "I've got an idea. Why don't you come over to our house to do your interviews NOW? Then I'll get you some photos for your project as well."

(This isn't how I wanted to spend my weekend at all.) I'm about to say, "I'm fine, thanks, Uncle Kevin," when Mum comes back, and she only goes and AGREES with him.

"What a GREAT idea! You two can go ahead and I'll drop the drill round to your house once Frank's found it – he's still looking. I'll pick Tom up at the same time. That would work for all of us, wouldn't it?"

(No, not for ME.)

I'm guessing Dad's **lost** the drill and needs more time to find it.

"At this rate, Tom, you'll have your whole project done in no time at all.

How good is that?" she asks me.

Hmmmm...

I'm overjoyed.

I collect up my stuff and then Uncle Kevin and I head off to his car.

"I'll see you later," Mum says to me, waving.

At the cousins' house
(Even though they're not here)

Uncle Kevin's car is a LOT cleaner than ours and he's got heated seats, which he asks me not to play with.

Please don't play with those buttons, Tom!

When we get to the house, he calls out,

ALICE, guess who's HERE!

Whoever it is, I hope they can put up PICTURES!

she shouts back.

(I can try?)

Aunty Alice looks surprised to see me. "Oh, hello, Tom. Your cousins aren't here, I'm afraid."

"I know," I say. Then Uncle Kevin explains.

"Tom's doing a project and he wants to interview us!"

"Is that before or after we put up the pictures?" Aunty Alice asks him.

Before, obviously...

Then I explain helpfully,

"Dad's still looking for the drill at home."

"I think he's lost it, which is typical," Uncle Kevin adds.

"We could just use a hammer and nails. It might be easier," Aunty Alice suggests.

"I better get those photos for Tom..." Uncle Kevin says, and disappears like he doesn't want to put up pictures at all. I have to stand there feeling a bit AWKWARD until Aunty Alice has a very good suggestion.

"Would you like a drink or a snack, Tom?"

(Silly question, really.)

Both, please!

The good thing about coming here is there's always an excellent selection of treats, and today is no exception.

Even better, I get to pick what I want first as the cousins aren't here. (But I am very nice and leave them the fruit.)

Uncle Kevin has got out the photo album to show me, so I let them have a look at the FAMILY TREE I've done (so far).

"Right, Tom – let's answer some of your questions, shall we?" "Let's... "

In between mouthfuls of wafer, I find out that Aunty Alice's hobby is collecting pebbles and painting different birds on them. (Random.)

"What kind of birds do you paint?" I want to know.

"I'll show you!" Aunty Alice goes to get a selection of what she thinks are her best **STONES**.

I've seen some around OUR house, but I didn't know Aunty Alice made them. (I might even have played with them.)

Let battle commence.

She brings the **STONES** back on a pillow and tells me, "They're very precious and take a long time to make. We keep them nice and safe so they don't get chipped or damaged. I've given a few to your mum and dad," she adds.

"I've never seen them!" (I think I have.)

CLUNK CLUNK Take That

Who knew?

Uncle Kevin gets out some photos he thinks I might be interested in. There's one of him and Dad when they were at school, and Uncle Kevin's holding a VERY BIG trophy.

"What's that for?" I ask him.

"I won MOST IMPROVED at sports."

 "Is that a good thing to win?" I wonder.

"It was a trophy, so I was very happy," he explains.

"You can't tell," I say.

"I also learnt an important life lesson that day."

"Was it 'don't hold a trophy in front of your face when you have your photo taken'?"

"No, Tom. This photo represents a crucial moment when I learnt how to deal with the crushing disappointment of <u>NOT</u> meeting my footballing hero, Brian Cliff."

"OK... So how comes my dad looks almost happy?" I ask.

"Your dad was just pleased to get the day off school!"

(I get that.)

"You should put this story in your project. I'll tell you exactly what happened."

(I grab another snack as this could take a while...)

It does...

"Will Dad remember this photo?" I ask when he's finished.

"I think so!" Uncle Kevin lets me keep it for my project, along with a few other pictures too.

Then Aunty Alice and Uncle Kevin finish answering my questions, which means I'm all ready to go when Dad comes to pick me up – WITH a POWER DRILL.

"I thought I'd bring it myself," he says, handing it over. "I'm sorry about the delay – it was buried under a box of other things!"

"Thanks, Frank! Oh hang on! It's still got a price on it," Uncle Kevin says. (Dad pretends not to hear.)

"Thanks, Frank. We could have just used a hammer and nails!"

"**NOW** you tell me!"

Uncle Kevin is already checking the drill over. "This is BETTER. Anyway, we've had a GREAT TIME, haven't we, Tom?"

We have!

"It's a shame your cousins weren't here. They'll be sorry to have MISSED you."

"I think they'll be **more** sorry about missing the good snacks!" I point out, which makes everyone LAUGH because they know it's true.
(I left fruit for the cousins.) One each

On the way home I tell Dad the story that Uncle Kevin told me and he can't stop LAUGHING.

I'm not sure WHY?

a! Ha! Ha! Ha! Ha! Ha! Ha! Ha! Ha! Ha! Ha!

He's still LAUGHING when we get home.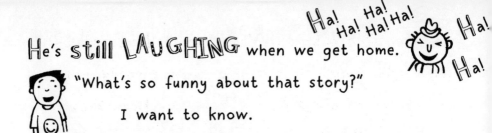

"What's so funny about that story?"
I want to know.

"Kevin's version isn't EXACTLY what really happened," Dad tells me, which sounds VERY interesting, so I show Dad the photo.

"Uncle Kevin said I could use it for my project," I say, which makes Dad LAUGH again.

"Let me tell you about that photo!"
Dad says as I get ready to take notes.

He chats away telling me EVERYTHING that happened and LOTS of other stuff too.*

*If you can't wait, see page 200 for the whole story.

I even find out how Mum and Dad met, which is also quite funny (if you skip out the soppy bits). I'm going to ask Mum the same questions because HER side of the story might be different to Dad's. (I BET IT IS!)

To make sure Mum and Dad know how much **EXTRA** work I've done on my school project, I make a list of what I've done so far - along with a list of EVERYTHING I need to bring to school. Then I stick it on the fridge where they'll see it. Mum and Dad will INSTANTLY be proud of me and probably want to give me treats.

(That's my plan.)

We're so proud.

Treats for you...

On top of the fridge, I suddenly notice a tin of mini caramel wafers (NOT very well HIDDEN). I'm hoping they are for ME! (My "well done, Tom" treat.)
I try not to get too excited. (For NOW...)

Mini wafers

Yum!

Back to School

Pleased

Knowing that I haven't forgotten ANYTHING as I walk to school with **D**erek is a **VERY** different experience for me. **THANKS** to **MY LIST.**

TOM'S
LIST
EXTRA WORK
I'VE DONE SO
FAR
Things NOT to
forget for
school.

My new **non**-rrrraassssping shoes are working out well – **D**erek thinks so too.

Nice quiet shoes!

Mum and Dad were VERY impressed with all the hard work I did at the weekend on my school project, which is **GOOD NEWS** for me as I get closer to eating those mini wafers.

Mini wafers

Yes!

"I'm sure Mum and Dad are saving them as MY TREAT!" I tell **D**erek.

Lucky you!

Derek has finished his BOOK and is even MORE

convinced that my grandparents could be SPIES.

 "In the story the SPIES travelled around

using their old AGE as a COVER-UP for

all their spying activities!"

"I'm DEFINITELY going to say The Wrinklies

are spies, then!" I tell Derek, as I might get

more merits for including interesting FAMILY facts.

In class I hand over my baby picture to

Mr Fullerman, who ONLY GOES and HOLDS it UP

for the WHOLE CLASS to see!

"Can anyone GUESS who this is?"

Everyone shouts out,

(Huh?)

IT'S TOM!

"You look exactly the same," AMY LAUGHS.

"You still have the baby drool too," Marcus joins in.

(It could be a long week. Sigh...)

My School Project

O ver the next few days we all work very hard to get our projects finished for the **OPEN DAY.**

I've added Marcus to my ✿ FRIENDS ✿ section as he's already put me in HIS project.

I didn't mind as it gave me the chance to write about my earliest memory of meeting him.*

I'm finding out all the time that some people remember things in VERY different ways

(like Marcus).

That never happened!

But the G O O D thing is, I've been able to write down all the most interesting BITS (including how my grandparents MIGHT be spies!)

*The whole story will be told on page 212...

170

My project has ended up being

(I think...)

FURRYTASTIC.

de-up
ord

AND I still have some stars and special { TAPE }
left over, which I'm sure I can put to
very good use on lots of other things.

BUT for now, please

Yeah!

ENJOY.

(Before)

Furry feature

(After)

When I grow up I want to be...

I've thought about this a LOT and decided that I would make an EXCELLENT spy. I have recently found out that there are TWO SPIES in my family already (keep that quiet). So I wouldn't be the ONLY one. The reason I would make a good spy is I am BRILLIANT at keeping secrets. (Unless someone is tickling me OR I'm really hungry and a wafer gets wafted under my nose. I'd BLAB pretty fast then.)

I'll talk.

Ha!

Ha! Ha!

My lips are sealed.

I'll talk.

But with practice, I'd learn to RESIST. I've kept LOADS of secrets to myself. Some things I haven't even told Derek about, and he's my best friend.

I didn't tell him for **AGES** when Dad sold Mum's VERY precious cat 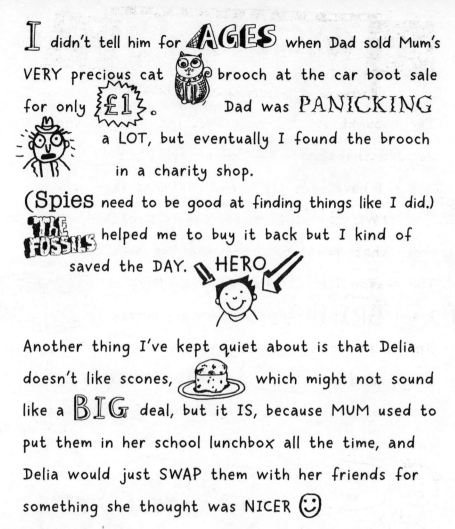 brooch at the car boot sale for only £1. Dad was PANICKING a LOT, but eventually I found the brooch in a charity shop.

(Spies need to be good at finding things like I did.)

THE FOSSILS helped me to buy it back but I kind of saved the DAY. HERO

Another thing I've kept quiet about is that Delia doesn't like scones, which might not sound like a BIG deal, but it IS, because MUM used to put them in her school lunchbox all the time, and Delia would just SWAP them with her friends for something she thought was NICER 😊 (which was anything).

Swap that pine cone for a scone.

Sometimes she'd even give them to ME, but I LOVE scones so that was OK.

Have it. Yum.

I also have **EXCELLENT** ninja skills that I've put to good use sneaking around school when I'm not supposed to be there.

I'm VERY good at eating crisps really QUIETLY, which might not seem like the best SPY SKILL to have, but I'm sure it would come in handy.

Crisps

I've lost him.

AND FINALLY I already have MY SPY name worked out. I'd call myself

Setag Mot.

(It's in CODE.*)

*See page 241 for answer.

My Earliest Memory

(A TRUE STORY)

One of my earliest memories was when Delia **BROKE** our T.V. screen and blamed it on me. Now I'm older it's NICE to be able to set the record straight.

Here's what happened.

I was only little and sitting on a nice soft rug playing with my toys. One of the toys was a ball. Dad had been rolling it to me and then I rolled it back to him. Delia was sitting on the sofa watching us, when Dad turned around to do something else. Delia took the ball and threw it UP into the AIR.

The ball landed on a VASE ...

... which toppled over into the TV screen.

There was a dull THUD as the vase hit the screen and a **crack** slowly appeared. It got bigger as it travelled up the glass and that's when Dad turned around.

"Oh no! Tom, what happened here?" he said, looking at the T.V.

Delia pointed at ME and said, "Tom threw my ball."

I was more CROSS that she said it was HER ball.

So I said, ⟹ ME! ME! When I should have said, "MINE!"

Dad thought I'd thrown the ball and Delia just kept quiet. She'd probably deny EVERYTHING - even now.

But I know what REALLY happened and so does she.

THE END.

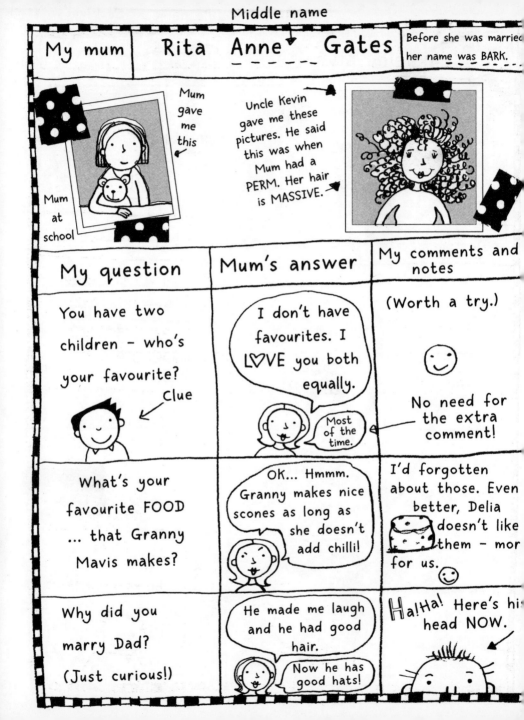

Middle name

My dad | Frank Daniel____Gates

Uncle Kevin said he held the balloon over Dad's head to make his hair stand up. →

Dad as a baby - crying a lot ←

My question	Dad's answer	My comments
You have two children - who's your favourite? Clue	"Ha! Nice try, Tom. We love you both."	I'll ask this again next time Delia does something they get cross about.
What did you want to be when you grew up?	"Good question! I wanted to be in a BAND and I also wanted to be a train driver."	(Train driver? That's a surprise.) He never told me he wanted to be in a BAND.
Who would win in a race - you or Uncle Kevin?	ME, obviously! Unless... Uncle Kevin cheats. Which is possible.	I bet Uncle Kevin thinks he'd win!

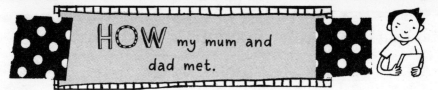

HOW my mum and dad met.

When I interviewed my dad, he told me how he first met my mum. I asked Mum **HER** side of the story too (which is a bit different from Dad's). I've missed out the SOPPY BITS because no one wants to read that stuff. YUCK. (TRUST ME.)

Here's a picture of Mum that shows what she looked like THEN.

Here's Mum now.

She hasn't changed much, mostly because she has all her own hair. (Unlike Dad.)

Here's Dad THEN.   Here's Dad NOW.

He wears a hat to cover his BALD head.

(He has a few hairs.)

A long LONG LONG time ago (because my parents are ~~VERY~~ quite old) Dad worked for a company as a junior designer, and Mum did a very important job, but I can't remember what it was – probably something to do with TAXIS, because THAT'S what she does now. Mum's always on her computer and the phone.

Hello... It's about your taxes.

Anyway, back to the story...

Their offices were next door to each other.

Mum's fancy-pants one

Dad's small office

afe where they met

CAFE

They both ate lunch in the nearby cafe and that's when Dad noticed Mum. Mum would order a healthy lunch like a SALAD – that kind of thing. Dad didn't like salad – he liked sausages, chips and beans. (Me too!)

Dad thought if he ate the SAME food as Mum she'd notice him and think  they had something in common! (How SAD is THAT? VERY.)

Like this
Mum taking NO notice
Salad
SALAD for ME please!
Not today...
No sausage, chips and beans today?

So EVERY time Dad saw Mum, he'd order a SALAD or something healthy and then try to say

Hello to her.

Mum told me she'd say hello back, BUT had no idea Dad was trying to impress her with his lunch choices.

Sigh... Eventually Dad got fed up of eating salad and decided to just ask Mum out instead.

At THIS point I SHOULD be saying:

And the rest is HISTORY.

But there's more.

When Dad asked her out, things didn't quite go to plan. He said,

Would you like to out for dinner tonight?

(This bit's funny)

Then Mum started to say...

No... I'm not...

And Dad thought she was saying NO to him and didn't stick around to HEAR the rest of her sentence.

(NOT listening properly still happens a LOT in our family.) Mum told me she was going to say,

No... I'm not FREE tonight, BUT let's go out tomorrow instead.

But she never got the chance.

If it wasn't for the cafe owner, that might have been the END of the STORY. (It's NOT.) He saw what happened and TOLD Mum where Dad worked. Mum wrote a note and put her phone number on it. Then she bought a slice of CAKE and put them both in a BOX and took it to his office, where she left the cake (and note) for Dad.

BUT someone else ATE the CAKE and threw the BOX with the note away. IN A BIN!

Mum was expecting a call to at LEAST say,

"Thanks for the cake..."

That didn't happen.

She heard NOTHING.

Dad was busy AVOIDING the cafe (and Mum). Then he went in (when Mum wasn't there) to get chips and the owner asked Dad if he'd got the NOTE and CAKE that Mum sent.

Dad wanted to know. This was <u>all</u> news to him.

Then he PANICKED and rushed back to his office to try and at least find the BOX, which had been thrown into the BIG outdoor BIN ➜ (that smelled).

Eventually he found the note and called Mum up pretending he'd been really BUSY.

So busy!

(He hadn't.)

They FINALLY went on a date – but I'm NOT writing about THAT bit. YUCK...

Mum and Dad got married, then they had Delia first and ME next, their favourite child. (Mum and Dad never SAY that, but I'm not as grumpy as Delia so I don't have much competition.)

THE END

No. 1

Here are some other photos Uncle Kevin said would be VERY good for my school project — ESPECIALLY as it has **FURRY** creatures in it.

I AGREE!

I never knew that DAD had so many different hairstyles when he was younger (and when he had hair).

Dad looks a bit like Delia here!

Uncle Kevin said they were at a wedding and Dad wasn't that pleased with his outfit.

Ha! Ha!
(I can see why.)

Can you GUESS who these two are?

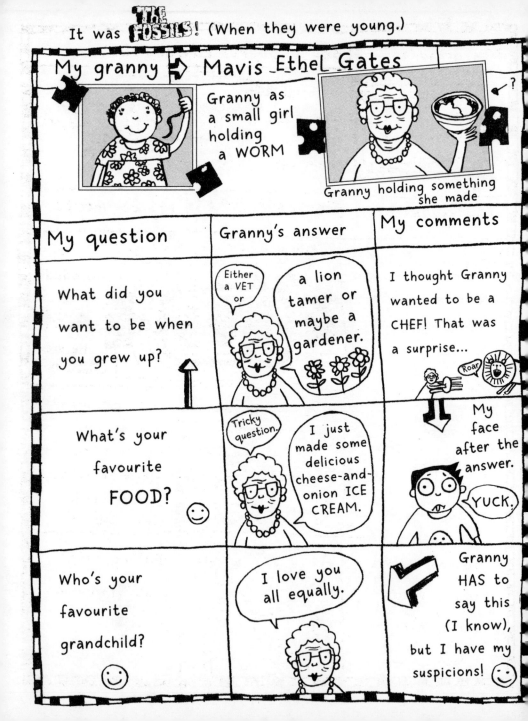

My other grandparents travel a LOT, so I don't really know them that well. But from what Mum and Dad (and Delia) have been telling me, they sound interesting. (Swimming with sharks, jumping out of planes – that kind of thing.) I found this postcard so I'm sticking it in because Derek thinks there's a reason they travel all the time.

(See next page.)

Hello!
Someone has promised to take this ashore and post it, so I hope it gets to you! We're still on a boat having wonderful adventures. We've learnt how to scuba dive and do martial arts, which might come in handy one day. You never know. See you very soon,

To: The Gates family

Love Granny and Granddad.

Reading this postcard makes me think that **D**erek could be right about them being ... **SPIES**. I'm going to leave some space in my **project** in case they come home, as I'll be able to ask them questions and write down any GOOD stories.

Though some answers might have to be

TOP SECRET.

I can blank things out like this:

My granny's pet is a ▆▆▆▆ and she went on a special ▆▆▆▆ where she ▆▆▆ ▆▆▆▆ and it all went very well. Her codename is ▆▆▆▆.

(That way no one will know any important secret stuff.)

Spy

The Wrinklies

(My other grandparents)

Empty space for any interesting FACTS I find out about them. (If they come home.)

If they don't have anything good to tell me, like this — then I'll use the page for doodling instead.

See →

Here's a photo of Uncle Kevin and my dad at school. They both have different versions of the SAME STORY. Here's what Uncle Kevin told me.

Uncle Kevin's Story

(In his OWN words – imagine he's talking [AT] you.)

"I was very proud of winning the 'MOST IMPROVED at Sports' trophy, and looking forward to picking it up from the WORLD-FAMOUS footballer Brian Cliff. He was going to present it to me at the NEW sports centre, which was a HUGE honour and I was very excited to meet my hero.

"My little brother Frank (your dad) was allowed to come with me as both our parents had to work that day. Frank was supposed to be helping out by taking a few photos of me with the trophy, only he forgot the camera. (That was the FIRST thing that went wrong.)

We got on the bus nice and early so as not to be late, looking all smart and ready for the ceremony. Then I noticed a group of NOISY kids who were messing around and being very silly. I told Frank to stay at the FRONT of the bus to AVOID them.

We watched as the kids KEPT pressing the BUZZER and making the bus STOP.

It was going PING! PING! PING! and the bus driver wasn't happy at all.

You lot, stop pressing the bell!

"'If ANY of you do that AGAIN, you'll be getting OFF this BUS!' he told the kids, who carried on LARKING around. Frank and I tried to keep away from them as much as possible. But they only went and PRESSED the buzzer

AGAIN.

Oh no!

The driver STOPPED the bus, got out of his seat and said, 'RIGHT! THAT'S IT – I've had ENOUGH of your NONSENSE!' Then he told the kids to get OFF and wait for the next BUS. I didn't think he meant ME or Frank. BUT HE DID! I tried to tell him he'd made a MISTAKE. 'It wasn't US!' I shouted. The driver didn't listen – he made all of us get off and wait for the next bus, which took AGES. None of the noisy

BYE BYE.

kids admitted to pressing

the BUZZER.

"I was SO LATE that I missed the WHOLE prize-giving ceremony, and WORSE than that, I MISSED Brian Cliff, who had to leave for another appointment.

I was GUTTED! The teachers gave me my trophy, but it wasn't the same.

Frank went to take a photo but, as he'd forgotten the camera, someone else took one when I wasn't concentrating. Frank looks happier than me. I was pleased too, but that day was supposed to be FANTASTIC and it didn't turn out that way at all."

THE END

It's not the MOST interesting story, until you read my dad's version - then it gets better.

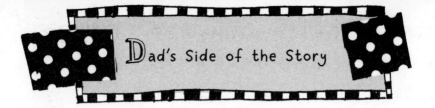

Dad's Side of the Story

(In HIS OWN WORDS.)

"I was SO happy to be out of school for the morning that I didn't even mind being bossed around by Kevin. We were going on the bus EARLY to a special ceremony where Kevin was being presented with a sports trophy he'd won for something not very impressive. I'd been given a camera to take photos, which was a good idea, but I left it at home (I only found that out later). I'd never heard of Brian Cliff (the footballer), but Kevin was a HUGE fan and wanted to make sure we were on time. When we got on the BUS, Kevin told me to avoid a noisy group of kids who he thought looked a bit ROWDY. I didn't think they were that bad ...

... until they KEPT pressing the BUZZER to make the bus driver STOP. Not just once but LOADS of times. I had to hold on to the pole really tightly to not fall over.

After about the TENTH time they pressed the BUZZER, the bus driver LOST it and told them ALL to get off and wait for the next bus. It was only when I LET GO of the pole and moved my hand that I realized it must have been ME who'd been pressing the

Oh...

BUZZER THE WHOLE TIME.

"I kept very quiet and didn't make a fuss when the driver made US get off too. Kevin was really cross because the next bus was late and he ended up missing Brian Cliff. I felt pretty bad that I couldn't take a photo either. I hope he'd see the funny side of things now, all these years later." ☺

The End

How funny is Dad? (VERY.)

I drew him his own trophy

BEST STORY

This part of my project is **all** about

YO!

MY

FRIENDS

(Not all of them, as that would take too long.)

I had to add Marcus as he only went and put ME in his project. Though it did give me a chance to remember how we first met.

Name	Amy	Jay	Porter	Another middle name!

I don't have a baby picture of Amy, so I made her name furry.

AMY

Amy's school photo (she gave it to me).

My question	Amy's answers	My comments
What's your earliest memory?	Being sick on my mum.	I wasn't expecting THAT answer.
Tell me a good joke.	What animal can jump higher than a building? Any animal - buildings can't jump!	Ha! Ha! Small building
What's your favourite snack?	Toasted cheese sandwiches.	Not exactly a snack - but I get it.

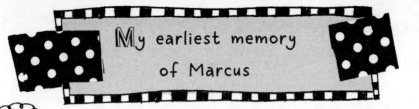

My earliest memory of Marcus

I first Met Marcus Meldrew at nursery school. He looked pretty much the same as he does now, only smaller and maybe slightly less grumpy. Marcus started nursery a few weeks later than everyone else (I don't know why), so the other kids had got to know each other a little. When Marcus was introduced to the class, he stood next to our teacher, Ms Tickly (that really was her name), while she said,

"Everyone, this is MARCUS MELDREW, who is joining us today!"

Hello...

We all waved and said hello.

Then she told us we should be REALLY nice and welcoming to Marcus and make him feel HAPPY to be here as he didn't know anyone yet. Which would have been a LOT easier for me to do if he hadn't gone and PINCHED my COAT HOOK!

Mine had a picture of a

SPACESHIP on it. I picked it out specially because it looked EXCELLENT.

Marcus thought so too and just went and helped himself to {MY} HOOK!

Huh?

Obviously I went and told Ms Tickly straight away that the new boy had made a TERRIBLE mistake and only gone and taken MY spaceship hook.

Ms Tickly said, "Oh dear..."

THEN she took me aside and said it would be REALLY kind and thoughtful, especially as it was Marcus's FIRST day, if I would let him KEEP the hook, and she promised to find me another one. "It will be JUST as special as the spaceship, Tom — would you mind?"

I said, "OK." But inside I minded a lot. When Ms Tickly showed me my NEW coat hook, things got worse. It was a picture of a CARROT and <u>not</u> even NICE one. ⟹

I was only little but even I knew that a carrot was not a good swap for a **SPACESHIP** (EVER). Unless you were a rabbit. (I would have preferred a rabbit for my hook.) I looked at the carrot and decided the only way to make the carrot better was to ...

... draw a face  ON IT!

Which made the carrot look a LOT better.
(I thought so, anyway.) I was standing back
admiring my drawing when Marcus Meldrew wanted
to see what I'd been doing.

 "You'll get into trouble for drawing
on that hook," he told me.

(I hadn't thought of that.)

"I won't tell anyone," I said, not wanting to get
into trouble. I wasn't banking on the NEW
BOY blabbing to Ms Tickly quite so fast.
Ms Tickly said I could keep the hook and my drawing
on it, but I mustn't draw on anything like that again.
I agreed. Lots of kids liked my carrot face hook and
 told me I was good at drawing – so that was
nice. When I asked Marcus if he remembered
pinching my coat hook at NURSERY, he thought
I was making it up! (Why am I not surprised?)

Since nursery school some things haven't changed. I still love drawing and Marcus can still be annoying. ➡ The End.

NOW FOR SOME

FURRY CREATURES

So many...

Made-up creature →

Here is a picture of my friend Derek's dog,
Rooster (who is already furry) with EXTRA fur for
no other reason than it made us LAUGH.
(You had to be there...)

Extra
fur is
actually
grass
cuttings

GUESS WHO?

Furry creature OR
Furry teacher?*

*See page 241 for answers

217

FURRY CREATURE FACTS

Chinchillas <u>don't</u> shed their fur.

When they are stressed or scared they have 'FUR SLIP' and lose it in clumps – here's what could happen.

Before
Cute furry creature

After
Boo!
← Fur clump

Chinchillas can also jump up to SIX feet in the air!

A house fly hums in the key of F.

A tarantula spider can survive for more than TWO YEARS without food.

Cats sleep for 70% of their LIVES!

Hmmmm

Hmmmm

Hmmmm

zzzzz

Thank you for reading my

SCHOOL PROJECT.

I hope I get a <u>LOT</u> of merits.

If my mum and dad are reading 🙂
this, some mini wafers would
be an excellent treat for
all my good work.

(Hint hint.)

SCHOOL OPEN DAY

Normally I'd try and put Mum and Dad off coming to an **OPEN DAY.** But this time I don't mind as most of my work is OK (and even FINISHED, which makes a change).

I think my school project might be the **BEST** thing I've EVER done in my **WHOLE ENTIRE LIFE** (at school).

Thank you.

Thanks.

The last few days I've noticed that Mum has been tidying up a lot more than usual.

Right NOW she's trying to take away my breakfast

Plump

before I've even FINISHED! I remind Mum that **OPEN DAY** is today, and ALSO that I'm a HELPER and staying LATE.

"I won't be coming home straight away, remember?"

Mum!

"What do you mean you're NOT coming home?" Mum says in a slightly SNAPPY way, until SHE remembers too.

"Oh yes - sorry, Tom. Of course, you're a helper."

Then Dad joins in and tries to be "FUNNY".

Over here, Tom!

"We'll see you in school, Tom.

I've got my YELLOW BIRD outfit

all ready so you won't MISS ME!"

(I know he's joking.)

"Ha! Ha! Funny, Dad," I say.

"We might have ANOTHER surprise for you,"

Dad says, winking at me.

"FRANK! We agreed not to say

anything YET," Mum says quickly.

WHAT SURPRISE? I ask. (Even though I

KNOW about the tin of mini WAFERS.)

"We're both looking forward to seeing your

project finished - that's all," Mum says,

cleaning up some more.

As I'm getting ready to leave for school, Delia walks past me. "Have Mum and Dad said anything to you about what's going on today?" she asks.

 "NO, what?"

"Doesn't matter – it's nothing. Oh, I just remembered. Dad said he's going to wear his yellow BIRD outfit to your school **open day**. Have FUN!" she LAUGHS.

"He's JOKING!" I tell Delia.

(I really hope he is. Dad better not come dressed up. I'm sure he won't.)

All the way to school I keep thinking about what Dad COULD be wearing. I didn't SEE any costumes around the house. UNLESS he's HIRED one for later?

That won't happen, I'm sure.

Being a helper for the **open day** stops me from thinking about Dad's possible costume SHAME.

It was a good idea to help out because I get to leave class early and wear an important BADGE ⇨ [HELPER TOM] and show NEW parents and kids around the school while telling them ALL about it. (Maybe not EVERYTHING.)

I explain about the school projects.

> This is where the school projects are displayed. It's also the dinner hall so it does smell in there. Feel free to look around.

I hang about a bit and notice that quite a few people and kids are READING <u>MY</u> project ... and LAUGHING! Which I think is a GOOD SIGN for future MERITS, and hopefully mini wafers too.

(Though I'm not sure which bit is so funny... Maybe the furry creatures?)

Ha!
Ha!

In between showing other parents and kids around school, I practise my SURPRISED face. "😃"

This is especially for when Mum and Dad FINALLY get to see my finished project. I'm HOPING they'll be SO HAPPY 😊😄 they'll INSTANTLY promise me the wafers when we get home. 😊

Then I'll say, 😄 "REALLY?" like I had NO idea they were for me, and do the FACE.

Like this → 😃 Wow!

Pansy Bennett brings more parents round and wonders WHAT I'm doing.

Are you OK, Tom? she asks.

"I'm FINE. 😊

Just HAPPY because my school project's done and DISPLAYED over there with all the others. Some projects are better than the rest,"

I add, because it's true.

Not ____▷ surprised   Surprised

224

As more parents come and go, Mr Fullerman joins us in the hall and starts chatting to everyone. When my Mum and Dad arrive I'm just pleased to see Dad's NOT wearing a bird suit. BUT STRAIGHT AWAY they both start talking to Mr Fullerman, who tells them...

"Tom's written some great stories for his project, and he's worked REALLY HARD – haven't you, Tom?"

"I have," I agree.

"It's FULL of interesting FACTS on your family," he adds.

"Oh good!" Mum says, looking at me and smiling.

"So LUCKY to find your BROOCH again, and how exciting to have SPIES in the family, TOO, isn't it?" Mr Fullerman says.

"What HAVE you been writing about?"

"Lots of things!" I tell them.

Mum and Dad look CONFUSED NOW and want to read my project.

I'm not sure if they're

enjoying it or not?

I needn't have worried. Mum and Dad weren't expecting to read so much about the family, but they do seem to like it (in the end).

Although Mum isn't HAPPY about her brooch and keeps saying, (You sold it for a pound?!) ... over and over again.

I think my school project is A HUGE SUCCESS! (Mostly.) Phew

On the way home Mum and Dad start asking <u>ME</u> more questions. Things like:

 "When exactly did you sneak into school and use your ninja skills, then?"

I manage to avoid answering by asking a question BACK to them.

"Are we getting a TAKEAWAY tonight for a special treat?" (Which works!)

"Probably - unless your Granny Mavis has cooked for us," Mum says.

"That's a good reason to GET a takeaway, isn't it?" Dad says. (He's got a point.) I'm still hoping the wafers will make an appearance as well. Though I am ready to do some more serious HINTING if I need to.

When we all get back THE FOSSILS are already there and they've made the house look really nice with flowers and the table laid out. It's like we're having a celebration all because of my GOOD ☺ school project, which they're VERY keen to see.

Who knew?

As they're reading it Dad says, "Maybe don't mention to Kevin that it was me who rang the bell on the bus all those years ago." Which they look surprised about.

We have to wait for Delia before we can order the takeaway – so for a change, I'm actually pleased to see her.

Here.

At last!

Now all we have to do is wait for it to ARRIVE!

Mum must be as hungry as I am, because every time a car or bike goes past she jumps up to see if the food's here.

When it does come, the *SPEED* she opens the door at is pretty impressive! Mum and Dad have ordered L**O**A**D**S more takeaway than we'd normally get.

(I'm not complaining.)

But Dad still SPOTS that his dish is missing.

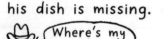 Where's my chicken?

"You can have some of mine, Frank. It doesn't look like we needed the extra food after all," Mum says.

I decide to tell EVERYONE that I'm going to leave some space just in case there are TREATS for AFTERS. (Like mini-wafer-sized treats.)

 "Especially for anyone who's done a very good school project," I add.

"You'll be lucky!" Delia says,

I hope she hasn't EATEN the wafers already...

Then Mum starts asking Delia why she never said anything about not liking scones, and while THAT conversation's going on the doorbell goes off again. This time Dad gets up. "That'll be my missing chicken dish, I HOPE!"

he says and goes out to get it.

"I LOVE scones with CHILLI!" Granny Mavis tells us. (No one else does.)

 Now Mum wants to know WHY I thought her parents were **SPIES.**

— Noodles

"Because Derek's got a book about **SPIES,** and everything the **SPIES** do, your parents do TOO! Travelling, swimming with sharks, being SECRETIVE..." I explain.

"I don't think that makes them **SPIES,** Tom!" Mum tells me as Dad comes back and interrupts us.

"Well guess what, everyone," Dad says. "You can ask them yourselves now..."

... and in WALKS ...

Two people I've never seen before.

"Hello, EVERYONE.
IT'S SO LOVELY to
BE HOME at last!"

It's only when Mum GASPS and starts hugging them that I GUESS it must be my OTHER grandparents - The Wrinklies.

"I didn't think you were coming!"

Mum says, followed by, "You both look SO different! Dad, you've got more HAIR!"

"Isn't it GREAT!" he says.

They don't look anything like their old photo. THE FOSSILS are happy to see them as well. Granny Pet and Granddad Joe tell me I've got so TALL and very HANDSOME (TRUE) and Delia has grown up a lot as well. Which is a nice way of saying she looks grumpy.

After this BIG surprise they come and join us for dinner and Granny Petula says they're going to stay for a while and RENT a house. Which is good news as it's my birthday soon so I might get double grandparent presents after all.

(I don't say that though.)

I do ask them what I think is a very important question. Everyone stops chatting to hear their answer.

"You know how you've both been away for so long? What I REALLY WANT TO KNOW IS ..."

"... HAVE you **EVER** tried a mini caramel wafer?

Because they are **REALLY**

nice and I think

you'd like them."

Delia groans, but I think it's important to show them all the things they might have missed out on being away so much.

I was right - they really do like them.

And I even show them how to do the wafer trick.

Which is the empty wafer?

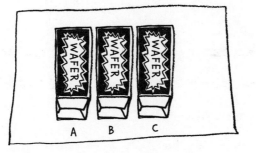

(I think it's going to be FUN getting to know my other grandparents before they go away again — if they do.)

Answer: it's C!

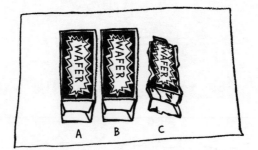

Furry creature band

Furry fans

Furry NOUGHTS and CROSSES

(I used some of
Marcus's tape!)

Class 5F baby pictures with names

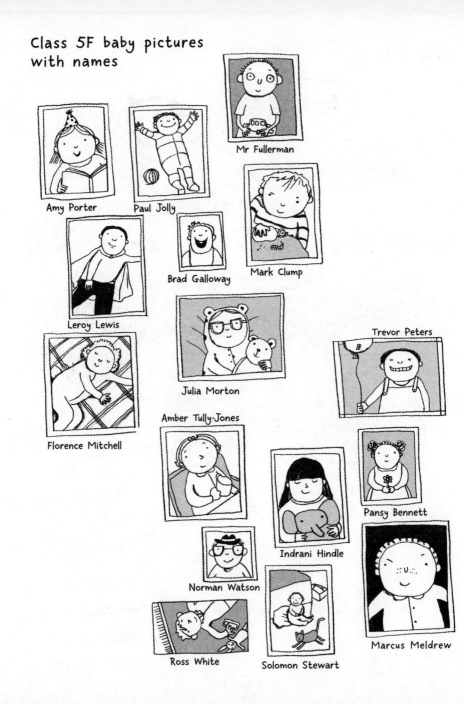

Amy Porter

Paul Jolly

Mr Fullerman

Leroy Lewis

Brad Galloway

Mark Clump

Florence Mitchell

Julia Morton

Trevor Peters

Amber Tully-Jones

Indrani Hindle

Pansy Bennett

Norman Watson

Marcus Meldrew

Ross White

Solomon Stewart

Page 178:

Setag Mot.

... is TOM GATES backwards!

Page 217: Furry creature or furry teacher?

Furry
Mrs Worthington

Furry Mr Sprocket

Furry creature!

If you want to do the MAZE on the
back — miss out the NEXT page!

Here!

When Liz 🧑 was little Ω, she loved to draw, paint and make things. Her mum used to say she was very good at making a mess (which is still true today!).

She kept drawing and went to art school, where she earned a degree in graphic design. She worked as a designer and art director in the music industry 🎸, and her freelance work has appeared on a wide variety of products.

Liz is the author-illustrator of several picture books. Tom Gates is the first series of books she has written and illustrated for older children. They have won several prestigious awards ⭐, including the Roald Dahl Funny Prize, the Waterstones Children's Book Prize, and the Blue Peter Book Award. The books have been translated into forty-one languages worldwide.

Visit her at www.LizPichon.com

Who doesn't love a photo booth?
Have YOU read All the Tom Gates BOOKS?
(I have — obviously.)

More Tom Gates stuff at
www.scholastic.co.uk/tomgatesworld/